Murder
in the Mist

Murder in the Mist

A STANLEY WATERS MYSTERY

WILLARD SCOTT

with Bill Crider

A DUTTON BOOK

DUTTON
Published by the Penguin Group
Penguin Putnam Inc., 375 Hudson Street,
New York, New York 10014, U.S.A.
Penguin Books Ltd, 27 Wrights Lane,
London W8 5TZ, England
Penguin Books Australia Ltd, Ringwood,
Victoria, Australia
Penguin Books Canada Ltd, 10 Alcorn Avenue,
Toronto, Ontario, Canada M4V 3B2
Penguin Books (N.Z.) Ltd, 182–190 Wairau Road,
Auckland 10, New Zealand

Penguin Books Ltd, Registered Offices:
Harmondsworth, Middlesex, England

First published by Dutton,
a member of Penguin Putnam Inc.

First Printing, January, 1999
10   9   8   7   6   5   4   3   2   1

 REGISTERED TRADEMARK—MARCA REGISTRADA

LIBRARY OF CONGRESS CATALOGING-IN-PUBLICATION DATA:
Scott, Willard.
    Murder in the mist : a Stanley Waters mystery / Willard Scott with Bill Crider.
        p.   cm.
    ISBN 0-525-94325-0 (alk. paper)
    I. Crider, Bill.   II. Title.
PS3569.C6896M85   1999
813' .54—dc21   98-26995
                                                                     CIP

Printed in the United States of America
Set in Cheltenham Light
Designed by Leonard Telesca

AUTHORS' NOTE

Higgins, Virginia, is a fictional town, and the Battle of Higgins never took place. However, Alexandria was in Federal hands for the duration of the Civil War, and a skirmish like the one described in the novel could have happened.

Murder
in the Mist

≈ 1 ≈

Men in Gray

"I think the uniform makes you look gallant," Marilyn Tunney said.

Marilyn was the chief of police of Higgins, Virginia, and Stanley Waters thought she looked a lot better in her uniform than he did in his. She didn't wear hers often, however. She was more likely to be dressed in a Donna Karan suit, as she was today, than her official outfit.

As for outfits, Stanley wasn't exactly sure what a retired weatherman, who now owned a bed-and-breakfast inn, was doing dressed like a Confederate soldier, anyway.

"You'll really get a lot of publicity for this stunt," Marilyn said, and Stanley suddenly remembered why he was dressed the way he was.

The battle reenactment hadn't been his idea, but when Barry Miller had suggested it, Stanley had seen the possibilities immediately. Barry was part owner of M & B Antiques and a passionate reenactor.

Or maybe that was a redundancy. In his brief acquaintance with reenactors, Stanley had yet to meet one who didn't have a passionate interest in what he was doing.

"It gives us a chance to travel in time," Barry had told him.

"We don't just put on uniforms and run around out there. We actually *become* people from another era. You should try it, Stanley."

Barry was so enthusiastic about reenactments that he was even growing an unflattering beard that spoiled his matinee-idol good looks and made him look at least ten years older.

At the time, Stanley had not had any intention of trying a reenactment of any sort. His change of mind had come later, after he had talked to Len Wilson, producer of *Hello, World!*—Stanley's old TV show.

Stanley was constitutionally unable to resist the idea of getting publicity for his inn, and while a Civil War reenactment on the grounds would be good, getting it onto network television would be even better.

Wilson liked the idea, too. "But not unless you're involved, Stanley. People still love to see you. That's why we invite you back to do a forecast every so often. And just think how much your fans would enjoy seeing you as a Confederate soldier."

So there Stanley stood, sweaty and gallant in his wool pants and jacket. He had on a muslin shirt under the jacket, but he couldn't tell that it was helping much. He had to keep telling himself not to scratch.

His haversack, slung over his right shoulder, was full of period items: coffee beans, hardtack, a Bible, and eating utensils. He had a cartridge box over his left shoulder, but that was empty, mainly because he didn't have a rifle.

Barry Miller had even tried to persuade him to order a musket from the Dixie Gun Works catalog.

"You can get a reproduction of a three-band Enfield for around five hundred dollars," Barry had said. "That's a rifled musket with flip-up sights and brass fittings. Fires a .577 minié ball and looks great."

But Stanley didn't want a rifle. "I don't think I'm going to make a very good soldier," he told Marilyn.

Marilyn disagreed. "Of course you are." She looked him over critically. "I especially like the hat."

Stanley removed the civilian-style hat, held it in front of him, and looked at it doubtfully. The hat was smashed and wrinkled and dirty, as if several thousand troops had marched across it with muddy boots.

"They told me it was supposed to look this way," Stanley said. "I think the soldiers sat on their hats to keep their rear ends dry, or something like that."

He put the hat back on, telling himself that he wasn't doing so because he was overly conscious of his bald head. Marilyn liked bald guys. Or so she'd said.

"Gallant, huh?" he asked.

"And stouthearted, too."

He was glad she hadn't stopped with just *stout*. He'd lost a lot of weight, but he still wasn't exactly what anyone would call svelte. He'd been svelte once, he thought, but that had been when he was around thirteen years old and had grown something like six inches taller in one year. Since then, *stout* was probably a much more accurate description.

"Of course you might look a little more authentic in another setting," Marilyn said.

They were standing in the parlor of Blue Skies, Stanley's inn. The parlor was decorated in the style of an earlier day, with most of the furnishings, including the big Philco radio, dating back to the 1930s.

"There were still some Confederate veterans around in the 1930s," Stanley said. "I don't think the last one died until 1959 or so."

"Maybe, but I just don't think the uniform goes with the radio, and the Battle of Higgins wasn't fought in a parlor. Why don't we go outside and have a look at you?"

Stanley wasn't sure he wanted to go outside, but Marilyn insisted.

"Let's go down to the creek," Marilyn said. "When we get back in the pines, we can almost forget it's the twentieth century."

Stanley liked the idea of going back into the pines with Marilyn. They had grown up together, even dated when they were much younger, but they had seldom seen one another since their long-ago graduation from Higgins High. Each of them had married, and their careers had led them in different directions.

Stanley had gone into radio and later into television, where as the weatherman on *Hello, World!* he had eventually become as well known as any public figure in America. His face was instantly recognizable to people from Maine to Alaska, from California to Florida. But after the death of his wife, he'd lost his taste for performing on a regular basis and moved back to his hometown, where Marilyn had gone into local law enforcement.

The murder of a guest at the opening festivities of Stanley's inn had brought them together again, and they had been seeing one another fairly often since then. Stanley had even helped solve the murder and in the process had gained a taste for investigation. However, crime wasn't exactly rampant in small Virginia towns, even if they weren't all that far from Washington, D.C., so Stanley hadn't had any further opportunities to practice his sleuthing skills.

He and Marilyn went out the front door of the inn, Stanley's authentic brogans clomping on the wooden boards of the porch. They left the porch and walked around back, past Stanley's garden, where Stanley had recently done his fall planting. He was sure that the rabbit that had plagued him in the spring was waiting eagerly for the fall crop.

Stanley followed Marilyn down to the creek and into the cool shadows of the trees. There were pines and cedars and plenty of dogwood trees, though the dogwood wasn't blooming now. In the deep shadows, with the sound of the little creek rippling in his ears, Stanley tried to imagine how a Confederate soldier might have felt.

He couldn't do it.

"I don't think I'm cut out for this," he said. "I feel more foolish than anything."

"You're not giving it a chance," Marilyn told him. "Try to imagine what it would be like to be all alone, separated from your unit. You can hear someone in the woods, but you don't know whether it's someone from your side or from the other. You don't know whether to hide, run, or just stand right where you are."

Stanley closed his eyes and tried to put himself in the place of the soldier Marilyn was describing, but it was no use.

"Maybe I should read *The Red Badge of Courage* again," he

said. "Or maybe you should have on the uniform. You're a lot better at this than I am."

"Don't be silly. You'll do just fine."

"Maybe. I wish I was as sure of that as you seem to be."

"You're a trouper, Stanley. You'll get into the part when you have to. Trust me."

"All right. If you say so."

"I say so. You'll be great."

And the funny thing was that she turned out to be right. Stanley did just fine, right up until the minute he got shot.

2

Prince Albert in a Can

Stanley had had every reason to think he'd come through the reenactment unscathed. Although several people had been shot in the original Battle of Higgins, reenactments were supposed to be much safer than the real thing. Otherwise, Stanley wouldn't have signed up.

He had learned about the original battle from his grandfather Waters, the same one who had told him the secret of properly curing and smoking hams, the one on whose farm Stanley had spent many happy summer days as a child.

Stanley had a number of vivid memories of his grandfather. One was the smell of Prince Albert tobacco, which came in a small red can that had a flip-up top and a picture of Prince Albert on the front. Another memory was the roughness of the old man's face. Grandfather Waters shaved only every two or three days, and his face was nearly always bristly.

Sometimes in the late afternoon when Stanley was visiting on the farm, he and his grandfather would go outside and sit on the front porch of the house in an old swing that was suspended by chains that hung from two hooks screwed into the ceiling.

Stanley would always ask for a story, and before Grandfather Waters began talking, he would fill his pipe with Prince Albert, light it, and get it going to his satisfaction, surrounding his head with smoke in the process. Then he would take the pipe out of his mouth, rasp his hand across his stubbled chin, and look out across the fields to where the sun was setting behind a hill.

Eventually he would begin talking in a quiet baritone that was only one of the things that Stanley had inherited from him. As often as not he would tell something about his childhood, but sometimes he would go further back and tell about things he had heard from his own grandfather.

Like the story of the Battle of Higgins.

"It wasn't much of a fight," he'd always say, his words accompanied by the squeak of the swing as it moved almost imperceptibly.

Stanley listened intently. In those days he had been eager to hear about battles and flying bullets, never dreaming that in fifty years or so he would be taking part in an attempt to make the battle live again. Or that one of the flying bullets would hit *him*. As a kid, he wanted the story of the battle to be lengthy and heroic, filled with startling events.

But in fact the so-called battle was hardly a skirmish to remember. It wasn't written about in books about the War Between the States (or "The Woah" as Grandfather Waters called it; you could hear the capital letters), except for the most thorough and painstaking histories, and it was remembered by the inhabitants of Higgins mainly because it was as close as the war had come to them. But it had been an offshoot of one of the most famous battles of all, a battle that had everything that Stanley wanted to hear about.

"It all started with First Manassas," his grandfather said, giving the battle the name it always had among Southerners, who would never have called it First Bull Run. Only Yankees called it that. In the days when Stanley was young, people like his grandfather, and even people considerably younger, still talked about The Woah as if it had happened only a few months ago, and their feelings about it were easily aroused.

"First Manassas was where Jeff Davis made his biggest mistake as president of the Confederacy," Grandfather Waters would always say, stating a belief that was shared by many of his generation if not by later historians. "Our boys could have whipped the Yankees for good and all right there. They had 'em on the run, and they could've followed 'em right back into Washington, D.C., and taken the city, but they didn't do it."

He'd puff on his pipe and look off into the distance, then continue talking almost as if he were talking to himself or to someone else that Stanley couldn't see.

"It was quite a fight, First Manassas. The Yankees thought they were going to run right over our boys, trample 'em into the dirt, and march straight on into Richmond covered with glory. Didn't work out that way, but that's what they thought. Why, people from Washington packed picnic lunches and piled into wagons and carriages and drove out to watch the Yankees win the war."

Stanley hadn't thought about it at the time, naturally, but the battle known as First Manassas had been a little like a reenactment: people had come to watch the fighting as if they were going to some sort of stage show on a gigantic scale. His grandfather had told him that there were women and children among the crowd, some of the women trying to watch the action through opera glasses.

"They didn't see much, I don't expect," Grandfather Waters said. "Just a white cloud of smoke floating up above the trees, since they stayed a good distance away from the fighting, sitting on the hill with their lunches and victory champagne. There were senators there, too, and some representatives. And reporters, naturally, plenty of 'em, writing about valor and whatnot. It was quite a party for a while. I guess they didn't think about the people who were fighting and dying under that big white cloud. Or maybe they just didn't know what was really happening."

The casualty figures from First Manassas had always amazed Stanley. Nearly four hundred Confederates had died in the fighting there, and another fifteen hundred or so had been wounded. Four hundred and sixty Union soldiers had died, with more than eleven hundred wounded.

And the really amazing thing was that the casualties were so low. Things got much worse later on.

"The air was thick with things flying around during that battle," Grandfather Waters explained. "Just like all the battles. Minié balls, wood splinters, grapeshot, cannonballs, rocks, and God knows what all. Stonewall Jackson was waving to one of his men when something hit him in his hand. Just a scratch, but then he was a lucky man at that time. You can still pick up minié balls and grapeshot if you walk around the battlefield today."

Stonewall Jackson hadn't been so lucky later on, as Stanley had learned in his history classes. But then a lot of people hadn't been so lucky in that war.

It was the Union troops, of course, who hadn't been lucky at First Manassas. They had fought well for a time, but surprised and overmatched by Southern reinforcements they hadn't expected, they had eventually begun to retreat.

"They turned tail and ran," is the way Grandfather Waters put it. "It was the civilians at first. They finally realized that it might be a good idea to get their precious hides back to Washington, so they jammed up the roads with their buggies and wagons, and then the soldiers started coming along with the artillery shelling 'em and our boys right behind 'em. It was a rout, and it wasn't a pretty sight. Women screaming. Congressmen trying to hide anywhere they could. Soldiers on the run."

One place the soldiers had run to was Higgins, and the result had been the so-called Battle of Higgins. A small group of Confederates had broken off to give chase to an even smaller group of Union soldiers who were fleeing north in what they hoped was the general direction of Washington.

It hadn't been, and the Union troops had found themselves on the outskirts of Higgins, where a number of the townspeople waited for them. The townspeople had been warned of the soldiers' approach by a farmer whose name was Sandstrom, and with him out in front they turned out to meet the troopers. The townspeople were armed only with rakes and hoes and the occasional musket, but they were game for a fight.

They took up a position on the outskirts of Higgins in a wooded area that was actually part of the property Stanley had bought along with his inn. They waited there for the Union soldiers, who were fired upon when they came over the top of a gentle rise that some people called a hill.

"My granddaddy—your great-great-granddaddy—saw the whole thing," Grandfather Waters told Stanley. "Or a whole lot of it. He was a young fella then, probably not much older than you are right now, but he was out there that day with a rake in his hand. He said the Yankees fought mighty hard, but there weren't many of them, and our boys had the advantage on them, knowing the countryside and all. Some of them slipped around behind the Yankees, and that was all it took. They rounded them up and took 'em all to Richmond. All but two of 'em. They were shot dead. They left those two in the trees."

Although he'd heard the story more than once, Stanley always asked the same question: "What happened to the bodies?"

"The townspeople buried 'em that very same day. Their graves are still there. I expect you've seen 'em."

Indeed Stanley had. They were a slight anomaly in what had become known as Higgins's Confederate Cemetery.

"Folks say their ghosts still walk around in those woods at night," Grandfather Waters went on. "Nobody knew their names, you see, and they're still roaming around, waiting for their markers to get a proper name on them. Don't go out in those woods at night, Stanley, or you're liable to run into those Yankee boys, still with their uniforms on."

Stanley would nod, and his grandfather would get up and lean over the porch rail to tap the dottle out of his pipe. Then they'd go in for supper, and Stanley would stay away from the woods for at least a week, night or day.

He should have stayed away for much longer, but there was no way he could have known that at the time.

≈ 3 ≈

Home Cooking

There was just one little problem with the reenactment from a strictly historical point of view. The Battle of Higgins had taken place in the afternoon, but Len Wilson wanted to get live shots of it for *Hello, World!* That meant the reenactment would have to be done in the morning.

"And we want you to come out beforehand, in your uniform," Wilson told Stanley. "Do the weather forecast for us. And you can do the local conditions as a prelude to the battle. I hope the sun is shining."

"It won't be," Stanley told him.

"How do you know?"

"I'm the weathermeister, remember?"

"Oh." Wilson was a good producer, but not exactly the sharpest quill on the porcupine. "But I thought you just got your forecasts from the National Weather Service."

"I do. That's the best way. Those guys have all the instruments and computers they need."

"So how do you know it won't be sunny tomorrow morning?"

"I listened to the local weather report this afternoon. On the radio."

Wilson laughed. The two men were sitting in the parlor of Stanley's inn, which held two radios, one of them the old Philco, and the other a modern reproduction that had AM and FM stereo, along with a CD and a tape player concealed within it.

"I still don't understand why you don't have a TV set in here," Wilson said.

Stanley shrugged. Television had done a lot for him, but he didn't want a set in the parlor.

"It wouldn't fit with the decor."

"Maybe not," Wilson agreed. "Anyway, fog won't be so bad. In fact, it might make things look even more real. Give it a touch of eeriness, too. You know—soldiers slipping through the early-morning mist like spirits of the Union dead."

Stanley thought about his grandfather's stories. "That's not something I'd joke about if I were you, Len."

Len grinned. "Sorry. I forgot for a minute how serious you Southerners are about your history. But don't worry. We'll do this right. You're going to get a ton of free network time."

Stanley thought that was just fine, though it wasn't as if his inn were hurting for patronage. He was already booked months in advance. But something in Stanley drove him to seek publicity. Even after he had become an established star on *Hello, World!* he had gone out and opened shopping centers, visited convalescent homes, marched along in front of high school bands, and emceed at balloon festivals.

The truth was that it really wasn't the publicity that mattered so much. Stanley just enjoyed being around people. He liked them, they liked him, and everyone had a good time, which was another thing that Stanley couldn't resist and which was another of the reasons he'd opened his inn in the first place. It wasn't as if he needed the money.

"Besides," Len said, "you can do all that other stuff in the afternoon: the farriers, the shooting demonstrations, the music, all that."

Stanley didn't go in for halfway measures. If he was going to have a reenactment, he was going the whole hog, which meant bringing in a lot of things besides just the re-creation of a battle.

"Are you sure you don't want to put some of that on the air?" he asked. "It's very educational."

"We'll tape it. We'll run parts of it all week on our 'Cruising the Country' segments. Schoolteachers love that stuff."

"Everybody loves it. It's the real thing. Living history."

Len was losing interest. "What did you say Ms. Caldwell is fixing for dinner?"

"You can call her Caroline. She'd probably be flattered. And I didn't say."

"Well, she's a wonderful cook. I'm sure whatever she has for us will be great."

That was an understatement. In Stanley's opinion, Caroline Caldwell was the best cook in Virginia, a state that prided itself on good cooking. She was a little temperamental, and as far as Stanley had been able to determine, her sense of humor was so small that it could have danced on the head of a pin. But he didn't mind. He would have put up with nearly anything to keep her on his staff.

"What she's having is smothered pork chops, stuffed zucchini, creamed potatoes, and homemade biscuits." Stanley's mouth watered at the prospect.

Len licked his lips. "I thought you went in for health food these days."

"Not all the time. We like to give the guests something that will stick to their ribs."

"I'm not sure the crew can take it. But I'll bet they'll try."

Stanley was sure they would, and he was right. In a short time, they were all gathered around the big dining table. In addition to Len, there were Grant Tyler and Lori Hummel, *Hello, World!*'s morning duo; Troy Dresser, the show's announcer; and Nancy Holden, one of the reporters. Caroline Caldwell and her husband, Bill, the inn's housekeeper, preferred to eat in the kitchen.

It was probably only Stanley's imagination, but the biscuits appeared to be so light that they seemed to hover in the air over the plate. They were served with real butter and with honey made from local flowers. With biscuits like that, you didn't need anything else, but that didn't stop anyone from eating the pork chops, the potatoes, or the squash.

By the time the last of the gravy had been sopped up, everyone was practically euphoric, even Tyler, who was one of the few people in the known world that Stanley Waters actively disliked.

It wasn't Stanley's fault, however. It was Tyler's.

From Stanley's first day on the set of *Hello, World!* Grant Tyler had made it clear that he was the star of the show and that Stanley wasn't. Stanley hadn't minded. After all, he knew he was only the weather guy, and he wasn't interested in seeing who got the most fan mail.

But Tyler didn't let up. Before long he had begun making snide remarks about Stanley's weight or his hair loss or his corny sensibilities. Stanley wouldn't have minded even that, really, if Tyler hadn't made his remarks on the air.

A typical moment: "And now, here's Stanley Waters with the weather. Hey, Stan, there's a little glare from over there. Did makeup forget to powder your head this morning?"

Among other things, Stanley didn't really like to be called Stan, a fact of which Tyler was well aware.

Another typical Tyler observation: "That was a great forecast, Stan, but we couldn't see the East Coast on the map. How many desserts did you have last night, anyway?"

Stanley, who had never done anything to Tyler, could never quite figure out why Tyler enjoyed attacking him. Stanley liked to think it was somehow connected to Tyler's insecurities. Tyler wore what had to be the worst toupee in the history of network television. Those who thought that television personalities had only the best of hairpieces had never seen Tyler, who often looked to Stanley as if he were balancing a squirrel atop his head—a squirrel that had made a quick, though erratic, run through a vat of hydrogen peroxide.

Stanley, on the other hand, had given up his own toupee years before. It made his head sweat and itch, and at times he found the temptation to raise it up and fan some air under it almost irresistible. So he quit wearing it, a move that endeared him to many viewers and brought in a ton of fan mail, fan mail that Tyler clearly resented.

As Stanley remembered it, the cutting remarks had started about that time, and they had gotten worse through the years. Although the death of his wife had been Stanley's chief reason for announcing his retirement from regular appearances on *Hello, World!*, Grant Tyler's attitude toward him had at least a little to do with it.

Lori Hummel was a different story. Stanley had always gotten along with her just fine. She was bright and funny and attractive in a wholesome, Martha Stewart sort of way. It was too bad, Stanley thought, that she was married to Lawrence Payne, a philandering actor who spent most of his time in California "auditioning" hopeful young women for parts on *The Faculty Lounge*, his mediocre sitcom set at a small liberal arts college where the major of choice among most of the student body appeared to be surfing.

Troy Dresser, who had attacked the pork chops with particular relish, had been in television for longer than anyone, even Stanley, could remember. He was one of the genuine old-timers who had come over from radio and had once been involved with such shows as *Fibber McGee and Molly* and *The Great Gildersleeve*. He had a mane of silver hair that he combed straight back and that Stanley envied tremendously. His voice, one of the most recognizable voices in America, was as rich and powerful now as it had ever been.

Nancy Holden had been at the inn before. In fact, she had been the network reporter on the scene during Stanley's opening ceremonies, on the day when the unfortunate Belinda Grimsby had fallen facedown into a bowl of salsa and died right there on the spot. Nancy was an intense brunette, and she hadn't appreciated Stanley's attempts to steer her away from the body in the salsa.

"I hope there aren't going to be any accidents or sudden deaths around here," Nancy said, just as Caroline came in with a fresh, hot apple pie.

"Don't worry," Stanley said. Belinda's murder wasn't something he liked to talk about at mealtime. Or any other time, for that matter. "Reenactments are completely safe. Nothing's going to happen except some good, old-fashioned excitement along with a solid lesson in American history. Now, who wants a scoop of ice cream on the apple pie?"

Everyone did except Grant Tyler. He wanted two.

≈ 4 ≈

Scripture

After dinner, everyone went into the parlor to listen to an old radio show. Stanley got out a tape of *Fibber McGee and Molly*, one where Fibber opened the closet.

"Were you on that show?" Len asked Troy Dresser.

"I just substituted as the announcer now and then," Dresser said. "I was never a regular."

After the show, Stanley put on an Ink Spots CD, but no one really seemed interested in hearing it. They all had to get up early the next morning to get ready for the show.

Troy Dresser, who'd known a couple of the original Ink Spots, hung around a bit longer than the others.

"Will you be carrying a gun tomorrow, Stanley?" he asked.

"No. I don't like guns."

"That's probably for the best. If you had one, you might be tempted to shoot someone. Like Grant Tyler."

Stanley was surprised. "What makes you think I'd do a thing like that?"

Dresser grinned. "I don't really think you would. But I'll bet he'd shoot you if he ever got the chance. He really doesn't like you, Stanley."

"Do you have any idea why?"

"Oh, he probably has his reasons."

Dresser looked as if he might have more to say on that topic, but he changed the subject to the Ink Spots, and when the CD had ended, he said that it was time for him to go to bed.

After Dresser went upstairs, Stanley sat in the parlor for a while, thinking about what Dresser had said. Dresser had been kidding about shooting Grant; although Stanley didn't much like Tyler, he had never considered retaliating against Tyler's insults. Stanley wasn't sure whether that made him a good person or just a sucker. He figured it was probably the latter, but it wasn't in his nature to retaliate or hold a grudge, at least not for long.

He got up, put away the Ink Spots CD, and went into the kitchen. Bill had finished the dishes, and he and Caroline had gone to their own apartment in the old servants' quarters behind the inn, not far from the barn. The kitchen was sparkling. Bill was almost as good a housekeeper as his wife was a cook.

Stanley left the kitchen and went to his own room, the only living quarters on the ground floor. There were no presidential portraits as in the upstairs bedrooms, but it was distinguished by the three cat baskets lined up against the wall. Binky and Cosmo were curled up in theirs, sound asleep, but Sheba was nowhere to be seen.

Binky, a huge gray tabby, had one paw thrown up over his eyes as if to shield them from the light. Cosmo, who weighed about one-third as much as Binky and was three times as old, looked up at Stanley and blinked once.

"Where's your sister?" Stanley asked him.

Cosmo yawned, stretched, purred loudly for about a second, and went back to sleep. Stanley had known the cat wouldn't answer him. He was just the kind of man who liked to talk to animals.

Besides, even if Cosmo could have talked, he most likely wouldn't have had anything to say about Sheba. He wasn't interested in Sheba or her whereabouts. Aside from eating and sleeping, he wasn't interested in much of anything as far as Stanley could determine.

Stanley wasn't worried about Sheba even though she wasn't

around. A cat door led outside from the back porch, and some-times the cats liked to roam around a bit in the evenings. The only place in the inn that they weren't allowed to go was up-stairs, and they didn't seem to care much about going up there, anyway.

After checking on the cats, Stanley looked over at the uni-form that was hanging on the back of the chair that sat in front of his rolltop desk. The top was open, and Stanley could see his notebook computer, a Compaq Presario that was already obso-lete though he'd had it less than a year and hadn't really learned to use it well.

Somehow the uniform didn't seem out of place there in front of the complicated electronic machine. Stanley had always felt that there were strong connections between the present and the past, and even though he was modern enough to use the computer to figure his accounts or check through his guest list, he nevertheless felt a powerful attachment to both his own past and the pasts of his ancestors.

He sat down on the bed and pulled off his shoes, remem-bering as he did so his grandfather Waters and the stories he'd told. His grandfather had been born less than twenty years after the end of the Civil War and had lived through a small portion of the nineteenth century. Stanley had known him, talked to him, heard his stories. And Grandfather Waters's father and grand-father went back further still into the country's history in an unbroken line, all the way back to the Civil War and even be-yond that.

Stanley shook his head. It always amazed him to think that he had grown up knowing a man who had been born over a hundred years ago. And that man had grown up with and talked to people who were born over a hundred years before his own death.

When you thought about it one way, a couple of hundred years seemed like an awfully long time. But when you thought about it in another way, it wasn't long at all, no more than the lifetimes of four or five men whose blood still ran in Stanley's veins.

As Stanley brushed his teeth and got ready for bed, he thought about those men and all the things they had seen and done. And about what he would be doing in the morning. He would be putting on the uniform, much as his great-great-grandfather had done, and going out to fight the Yankees.

Well, there would be one big difference. Stanley wouldn't be carrying a gun.

After putting on his yellow pajamas, Stanley sat in the rocking chair and opened his Bible. He liked to read early in the mornings and before going to bed. He read all kinds of things, from mystery novels to science books, but somehow he thought that something from the Bible might help him relax.

He turned at random to the book of Deuteronomy and started reading in chapter twenty. It wasn't long before he realized that he was reading the rules of war, some of which discussed who should go into battle and who shouldn't.

He found himself especially interested in verse seven: "And what man is there that hath betrothed a wife, and hath not taken her? Let him go and return to his house, lest he die in the battle, and another man take her."

Stanley found himself thinking about Marilyn Tunney, and the top of his head began to turn red. He wasn't betrothed to her, after all. They were more than good friends, true, or at least he hoped they were, but certainly there was no reason for him to be thinking what he was thinking. He was reading the Bible, for goodness sake. Still, the top of his head kept on getting hotter and hotter.

Better go on to the next verse, he thought, and read verse eight: "And the officers shall speak further unto the people, and they shall say, What man is there that is fearful and fainthearted? Let him go and return to his house, lest his brethren's heart faint as well as his own heart."

Stanley wondered if that verse was aimed at him. He certainly didn't look forward to going into battle, and he wondered how he would feel when the rifles started firing and the smoke filled the air.

He remembered having read *The Red Badge of Courage* many years ago for a high school English class. The young soldier in the book, Henry something or other, had turned and run when his first real test of battle had come.

Stanley hoped he wouldn't do the same. He closed his Bible, almost sorry that he had opened it. What he had read wasn't exactly calculated to help him relax.

He put the Bible on the desk, glanced at the cats again, and turned off the light. As he got into bed, he found himself smiling, and then he laughed out loud. He had put himself into the place of a real soldier. He was thinking as if he were actually going into a real battle. Barry Miller would be proud of him. He was getting into the spirit of the reenactment much better than he'd thought possible.

Stanley was still smiling to himself when he fell asleep.

He was awakened sometime later by the sound of something scuffling on the stairs.

Sheba was coming in, he thought, before he drifted off again.

Into each life some rain must fall,
Some days must be dark and dreary.

—Longfellow, "The Rainy Day"

Rise up, my love, my fair one, and come away.
For, lo, the winter is past, the rain is over and gone.

—The Song of Solomon 2:10–11

⪜ 5 ⪝

"Just Before the Battle, Mother"

Stanley had been an early riser ever since one of his first jobs in radio, when he had to be at the station and on the air to give the farm report long before daylight. So it was easy for him to get up the next morning at four-thirty and put on his uniform. He could hear some of the TV crew shuffling around above him, but he was the first one into the kitchen for breakfast.

Caroline wasn't accustomed to getting up quite so early, but she was there, and the kitchen was filled with the smells of coffee, bacon, sausage links, eggs, toast, and hash browns. Caroline poured coffee into a thick mug and fixed a plate with a little of everything and put it on the table.

"That uniform fits you nice," Caroline said.

"It doesn't make me look fat, does it?" Stanley asked.

"Not a bit. It kind of slims you down, if anything."

Feeling good about his appearance, Stanley sat down at the table and drank some of the hot black coffee. He didn't need the caffeine to get him started, but it did seem to perk him up a little.

"Did you know there were fires out there?" Caroline asked.

"Fires? Where?"

"Outside, down in the trees."

Caroline went to the window and pulled back the curtain.

Stanley got up and looked outside. "Oh. Those are camp-fires. Some of the reenactors like to camp out the night before they perform. They sing the old songs and tell old stories. It helps them to get in the mood."

He went back to the table and started working on his breakfast.

Caroline obviously wasn't an outdoors person. "All camping out ever did for me was make me cold and miserable."

"It's still pretty warm this time of year," Stanley said around a mouthful of eggs.

"But it's damp. Real damp. I'll bet everyone's blankets are soaked through this morning."

"I think they slept in tents. I'm sure they were fairly well protected."

"Not in this weather. That fog can come slithering in right through the smallest opening."

Stanley had forgotten about his forecast of fog. "You're proba-bly right. Well, no one ever said that soldiers were supposed to be comfortable."

"Soldiers," Caroline said. "Hah. A bunch of grown men play-ing games is what they are."

"It's not like that at all. They're reliving a part of history and making it real for other people to see. The battle isn't the only thing going on. There'll be a lot of educational exhibits out there today."

"I saw them setting up some tents yesterday, but it didn't look like anybody was going to sleep in them."

"That's Sutler's Row," Stanley said. "There'll be some peo-ple selling cloth and clothes in them today."

"Is anybody going to dance the Virginia reel?"

"I wouldn't be surprised."

"I'm pretty good at that myself," Caroline said. "But the bat-tle's the big event, isn't it?"

"That's right. We'll try to make it as realistic as possible."

"Not too real, I hope. Somebody could get hurt that way."

"It won't be dangerous," Stanley said. "No one's going to get hurt."

Caroline looked as if she wanted to contradict him, but just then Len Wilson walked into the kitchen.

"Is that coffee I smell?" he asked. "I'll take the biggest cup you have."

He sat at the table and began talking to Stanley about how he wanted the weather forecast for *Hello, World!* Then the others came in one by one to exclaim about how good the food smelled and how hungry they were.

No one mentioned danger again—or even thought of it until it was too late.

The makeshift studio in the barn worked out just fine. Stanley felt a little odd giving a forecast in a Confederate uniform, but he'd dressed in odder things in the past. He remembered one time when he'd put on a jester's outfit that Grant Tyler said was entirely appropriate.

Tyler was more restrained today, limiting himself to a snide remark about how much better Stanley looked wearing a hat.

"And it saves wear and tear on the powder puffs in make-up," he added. "Now, Lori, what do you have for us on the Health Minute?"

"It's all about broccoli, Grant," Lori said, smiling for the camera as Stanley unhooked his mike and left the studio.

It was well after daybreak, and the Northern troops were gathered on a hill a hundred yards away. The defenders of Higgins were waiting not far from Stanley's barn. They were all dressed pretty much as Stanley was in a sort of mixture of military and civilian dress, as befitted irregular troops.

Calvin Brooks, *Hello, World!*'s director, was with them, but it was Barry Miller who came to meet Stanley. His beard still hadn't been trimmed, but now it looked perfectly appropriate.

"Ready, Stanley?" he said.

Stanley looked around. The shadows were still deep among the pine and dogwood trees. The sky was overcast, and a thin fog hung in the air like a mist that seemed to be rising from the ground. An occasional slant of early-morning sunlight would find its way through the clouds and tree branches and turn the mist to smoke.

Stanley shivered in spite of himself. Although several camera-men were stationed in strategic spots, Stanley didn't find it hard at all to imagine that back among the trees the spirit of his great-great-grandfather was stirring around, waiting to see just how real the battle would look.

"I'm as ready as I'll ever be," Stanley said.

"You know most of the group, I think," Barry told him. "I'd introduce them, but most of them are already in character. We've only got about five minutes."

Stanley saw several prominent Higgins citizens. One was Neddy Drake, the manager of Mom's Crispy Fried Chicken, and the only man Stanley knew who claimed to have been abducted by aliens.

Another was Rance Wofford, one of the town's richest men. A relative newcomer, he already owned a number of the build-ings downtown, quite a bit of land all around the area, and sup-posedly had a huge fortune invested in the stock market. He had recently taken over the General Lee Hotel and planned to remodel it completely, so he might be considered one of Stan-ley's competitors.

And there was Burl Cabot, who owned an auto parts store. He was a large, powerful man, who looked to Stanley as if he could loosen lug nuts with his fingers. His uniform jacket seemed about to split at the seams.

"What's Lacy Falk doing over there?" Stanley asked.

Lacy was the owner of Bushwhackers, a local unisex beauty salon whose name always gave Stanley pause. She was a plain-spoken woman from Texas, and she liked to assure her female customers that if they wanted big hair, they had come to the right place.

She had covered her generous charms with something that looked to Stanley like pantaloons and a camisole. He wasn't quite sure because she had a jacket thrown over her shoulders. She was also carrying a small parasol, not that it was doing her any good at the present.

"That's a pretty skimpy outfit she has on," Stanley said. "What's the idea?"

Barry shrugged. "She says she's a camp follower."

"It was a little early in the war for camp followers, wasn't it?"

"Oh, no. There were plenty of prostitutes who came out with that crowd from Washington to watch the fighting at First Manassas. One of them could certainly have drifted back up this way."

Lacy walked over to them. She was wearing shoes that laced up well above her ankles.

"Damn, fellas," she said. "When're we gonna get this show on the road? A girl can't earn a livin' until the soldiers get their duty done."

"It won't be long," Barry assured her. "We'll be starting any minute."

"Well, you'd better. Where should I stand if I want to get on TV, Stanley?"

"Just look for the cameramen," Stanley said. "They'll be moving around."

"Then so will I," Lacy said, walking away with a flip of her parasol.

Stanley turned his attention back to the soldiers.

"Do you think Al Walker knows how to handle a gun?" he asked Barry.

Walker was a math teacher at Higgins High. He wasn't much more than five and a half feet tall, and he looked overbalanced by his musket.

"He'll be fine," Barry said. "He's fired black-powder weapons plenty of times without trouble. You don't have to worry about him."

"What about Duffy Weeks?"

Weeks's real first name was Harold, but he'd operated Duffy's Tavern for so many years that most people in Higgins had forgotten that the place was named for an old radio show. So Harold had become Duffy in everyone's mind. Rumor was that recently he'd been sampling his own wares.

Barry smoothed his beard. "Duffy's okay. Most of that stuff you hear about him isn't true. Besides, it's too early in the morning, even for him."

"And no one's shooting real bullets," Stanley said.

"Of course not. Nothing to worry about on that account. And of course a few of us aren't carrying muskets."

Stanley could see that. The hoes and rakes didn't look as if they could do much damage unless the fighting got to close quarters.

Calvin Brooks strolled over. "I hate to break this up, gentlemen, but it's time to get rolling."

"Follow me, Stanley," Barry said, and motioning to the others, he led the way back into the trees.

As they trotted along through the foggy mist, Stanley felt his canteen bumping against his leg and smelled the dampness of the grass under his feet. He looked ahead of him at the men with their rifles, their hats pulled low over their faces.

We're going out to meet the Yankees, Stanley thought, and when he looked out over the grounds of the inn, all the spectators gathered there seemed to him to be dressed in the proper costumes, as if they'd driven out from Washington to watch the battle and celebrate the victory. He wondered if any of them had brought cold fried chicken for lunch or if they carried champagne in their picnic baskets.

Then he thought about the Yankees, on the run from the fighting at Manassas, lost and trying to find their way to Washington but instead stumbling across a little band of irregular troops, most of whom had never fired their guns at anything bigger than a squirrel but who were determined not to let the Northern soldiers cause any trouble in their town.

Stanley wondered what the Yankees thought when the townspeople started firing on them. He wondered if they ever considered just throwing down their weapons and giving up, but he supposed they hadn't. They just wouldn't have thought that way, even though fighting meant that two of them would die there in a place they'd never been before, a place they probably hadn't even known existed until they blundered into it.

Two of them were going to die there in that place so familiar to Stanley but so strange to them. At that moment, it was easy for Stanley to believe his grandfather's stories about the men's ghosts, still at large, still hoping that someday their right names would be put on the stones that marked their graves.

For just a second, Stanley seemed to get a glimpse of two ghostly figures moving through the trees without a sound, their feet never touching the ground.

Among the trees with the cold mist on his face, Stanley waited for the shooting to begin.

What surprised Stanley more than anything else was the noise. Oh, he had known that the guns would be loud, but he hadn't quite realized exactly *how* loud. The sound seemed to bounce back and forth from the trunks of the trees to hammer his ears. In the space of a moment his mind was jerked back to the present, and he wondered why no one had warned him to wear earplugs. He suspected that everyone else was wearing them, but maybe no one had thought to tell him because he hadn't been planning to carry a gun.

The Higgins troops were crouched at the edge of the trees, taking cover behind their trunks as they fired on the Northerners, who were running down the hill toward them.

Even Stanley could see that this was a poor tactic indeed, even considering how long it took the men in the trees to reload, but the Northerners had been scared and disoriented, and they hadn't been seasoned troops. They couldn't be expected to behave like military geniuses.

For that matter, it didn't appear to Stanley that the Higgins men were exactly models of soldierly prowess. Stanley was crouched with the others, near where Rance Wofford stood half out of concealment to "reload," and it seemed to Stanley that Rance might get himself shot if he wasn't more careful.

For just a second Stanley imagined what a real soldier would have heard in battle. There would be the whine of the minié balls, the cries of the wounded, and—an earsplitting rebel yell just like the one Rance Wofford emitted as he ran from the trees. He had his rifle ready to fire, and he charged straight at the boys in blue.

At widely spaced intervals, several men brandishing hoes and rakes broke from the trees. They were also yelling. The men with muskets had slipped through the trees and gotten behind the hill. Soon the Union men would be trapped between the two groups, and the fighting would be over.

Stanley followed Wofford out of the trees, trying his own version of a rebel yell. It wasn't very satisfactory, and he told himself that Rance and the others had no doubt had much more practice than he had.

He tried again, and his voice cracked, sliding into an unpleasant falsetto. He felt like an adolescent whose voice was suddenly changing.

Rance Wofford looked back at him over his shoulder and laughed.

Stanley had to admit that he had sounded pretty funny. He began laughing, too.

And then somebody shot him.

6

The Nonwalking Wounded

It was as if someone had hit him hard on top of the head and then turned out the lights. Stanley was unconscious before he had any idea what had happened. One second he had been jogging along, listening to the yells and the firing, and the next there was nothing at all—no sound, no pain, just blackness.

The pain came along when he woke up. Marilyn Tunney was looking down at him, her face just a little bit fuzzy around the edges. His head was throbbing as if a little man were marching around inside it and beating a bass drum.

"Don't move, Stanley," Marilyn said. "The EMTs will be here in a minute."

Stanley blinked, and a small circle of the skull on top of his head fell off in the grass. Well, it didn't actually fall off, but Stanley didn't know that. It certainly *felt* as if it had fallen off. Stanley moaned, closed his eyes, and passed out again.

The next time he came to, a man he didn't know was staring into his eyes.

"He's awake," the man said. "Can you talk, Stanley?"

Stanley tried to ask how the man knew his name and whether anyone had found the top of his head. But all he could do was croak.

"Just relax," the man said. "We'll have you in the ambulance in just a second."

Stanley tried to say *ambulance*. It sounded more like *ummlunce*.

"That's right. It won't be long. How many fingers am I holding up?"

Stanley didn't think it was fair to be asking such hard questions of a man who'd lost the top of his head and whose brains were most likely leaking out into the grass. He tried to put his hand up and feel the leak just to make sure he was right about it, but he found that he couldn't move his arm.

Well, that was fine with him. He didn't really want to know, anyway. If a man's brains were leaking out, it was probably better to remain ignorant of the fact. What he really wanted to do was to close his eyes and drift away.

"Can you answer the question, Stanley?" Marilyn asked from somewhere just out of Stanley's line of sight. "How many fingers is he holding up?"

Well, if Marilyn wanted him to answer, he'd try. He tried hard to focus.

"Th . . . three."

"Very good," the man said, sounding as pleased as if Stanley had recited the first book of the *Iliad* without peeking at the text. "Now, tell me your name."

"Stanley."

"Last name?"

Stanley gave it some thought. "Wa . . . Waters."

"Great. And do you know what day it is?"

That was a tough one. It required intense concentration. Stanley almost went to sleep thinking about it, but he finally came up with the answer.

"Monday."

"And Monday it is," the man said happily. "You're going to be fine, Stanley. All right, guys, let's get him in the ambulance."

Stanley had the sensation of moving through the air, almost as if he were flying. He could see Marilyn's face, but it was bobbing around so much that it was making him dizzy. He closed his eyes and went to sleep.

* * *

When he next woke up, he knew almost immediately that he was in a hospital room. There were plenty of clues. The bed was uncomfortable, the air-conditioning was cranked down into the fifties, the walls were a "soothing" institutional bluish green, and Stanley himself was hooked up to any number of wires and tubes that ran to a machine at the foot of the bed.

Nothing about the situation was of the remotest interest to him, however, so he went right back to sleep.

He came out of it again, and this time Marilyn was there. She smiled at him, and he smiled back, or he tried. He wasn't sure his mouth was working properly.

"Hi," she said. "How are you feeling?"

He tried to say "not good," but it came out more like "no' goo'."

Marilyn seemed to understand him. "No wonder. Do you know where you are?"

"Hospital."

"That's right. It's in Alexandria. The one on Seminary Road. Do you have any idea what happened to you?"

"The top of my head fell off," Stanley said, or something that vaguely resembled it.

Marilyn laughed. "I can see that you haven't lost your sense of humor."

Stanley didn't see what was so funny. He wondered if the doctors could reattach the part of his skull that was missing. He wondered if anyone had even looked for it. He tried to explain his worries to Marilyn, who finally realized that he wasn't joking.

"None of your skull's missing, Stanley. Well, not much of it, anyway. It just feels that way."

"Then what happened?"

Marilyn's face turned serious. "Someone shot you."

Stanley wasn't sure he'd heard her right. He was still groggy, and he'd probably been given some kind of painkiller. The little man had stopped beating the drum.

"Now you're the one who's kidding," he said.

"I wish I were, but it's true. Someone shot you. It's not life-threatening, but you do have a mild concussion. The bullet took a little gouge out of the top of your head."

The little man hit the drum a lick or two just to keep in practice. Stanley moaned.

"Don't worry about it," Marilyn said. "The bullet didn't take much of your skull along with it. It just skimmed along the top. If you hadn't been wearing that awful hat, it might have been worse."

How humiliating, Stanley thought. Saved by an ugly hat.

"It hurts," Stanley said.

"I'm sure it does. But the doctors said that you're going to be just fine. You'll have to spend the night in the hospital, but you can go home in the morning."

"Ruined the day," Stanley said, thinking of the big plans he'd had.

"It did put a damper on things. Of course some people were pretty happy about it."

Stanley didn't have to guess who "some people" were.

"Grant Tyler," he said.

"Him, too. But I was thinking about Len Wilson. He said one of the cameramen was focused on you all the way. It was 'great television.' "

"Would've been better if I'd died."

"He didn't say that."

"Probably thought it."

"Maybe."

It was quiet in the room for a minute then. Stanley could hear the humming of the air-conditioning and the beeping of the machine at the foot of the bed.

"There's something I have to tell you, Stanley," Marilyn said after a minute or so.

Stanley didn't say anything. He was tired and didn't feel like talking anymore. He closed his eyes and waited.

"You weren't the only one who got shot."

Stanley's eyes came open. "Who else?"

"Rance Wofford. He was only a couple of yards from you."

Stanley remembered his attempt to imitate Wofford's rebel yell and the way Rance had turned and laughed.

"Is he going to be okay?"

"No. He's not going to be okay."

"How bad is he?"

"As bad as he can be."

Stanley wasn't sure what she meant. He thought he had an idea, but he hoped he was wrong.

"How bad is that?" he asked.

"He's dead."

⌒ 7 ⌒

Blue Skies Again

Stanley didn't get the rest of the story then. He just wasn't up to it. Marilyn told him that she was going to stay in the room for a little while longer but that she would have to leave soon.

"I have to work the case," she said. "If it were up to me, I'd stay here with you all night. I hope you understand, Stanley."

She touched his hand, and Stanley felt his face getting warm in a way that had nothing to do with his wound or any of the drugs that he'd been given, whatever they might have been. He would have told her that he was glad she could stay even for a minute, but before he could say anything, he was asleep.

The next day, Stanley was feeling a lot better and considerably more alert. He would have walked out to the car that Bill Caldwell had brought for him if the orderly had allowed it.

"You'll have to ride in the wheelchair," the orderly said. "Hospital regulations."

So Stanley rode in the chair, feeling slightly ridiculous with the stitches running down his scalp. He figured he looked a little like Frankenstein's monster. At least they'd let him change out of the hospital gown into the clothes Bill had brought. Nothing, absolutely nothing, made a person look more ridiculous than one of those so-called gowns.

"You'll need to make an appointment to have those stitches out," the nurse told him.

Stanley said he would and thanked her for reminding him. Then the orderly pushed him out of the room to where Bill Caldwell was waiting in the hall.

"Caroline said to tell you she was fixing a special lunch today," Bill said, walking along beside the wheelchair. "All your favorites."

Stanley wasn't sure what that meant except that there would be chocolate pie for dessert, but he was willing to be surprised.

"That's nice of her," he said. "What about the guests? Any cancellations?"

"Not a one. You'll have a full house tonight, so I hope you're up to it. The TV folks all left yesterday afternoon and went back to New York. They said to give you their regards and to tell you they were sure glad you were all right."

"Even Grant Tyler?"

"Even him. He didn't sound like he meant it, though."

The wheelchair arrived at the elevator, and the orderly reached past Stanley and pushed the DOWN button. The doors opened at once, and the orderly pushed Stanley inside the elevator. Bill followed.

When the doors had closed, Stanley asked, "What about the reenactment?"

"You mean aside from you and Rance Wofford getting shot?" Bill asked.

"Yes," Stanley said. "Aside from that."

"Well, it wasn't too bad. There were a lot of people there, and some of them didn't even find out what had happened until a lot later. They thought you and Rance falling down like that was just a part of the show, and they'd moved on to other things before the ambulances got there. I imagine they heard the sirens, though."

The elevator doors opened, and the orderly pushed Stanley through and down a short hallway. Then they were outside, where Stanley's black Lexus 400 waited. When they got to the car, the orderly allowed Stanley to get up and into the car on his own.

"Thanks for the ride," Stanley told him.

"You're welcome," the orderly said. "Nice car."

The Lexus was one of Stanley's few indulgences. He liked to be comfortable when he was driving.

This time, however, Bill got into the driver's seat, and they started back to Higgins. It was quiet in the passenger compartment. Stanley could hardly even hear the tires humming on the pavement.

As they went past the downtown area, Stanley got a glimpse of the George Washington Masonic Memorial that looked down on Alexandria from Shooter's Hill. Thinking about Washington and his war reminded Stanley of the reenactment.

"Tell me about Rance," he said.

"There's not much to tell," Bill said. "Somebody shot the both of you, and you were the lucky one."

Stanley reached up and gingerly touched the stitches with his fingertips.

"What happened when people found out he was dead?"

"The TV folks went nuts. It just about made their day, I can tell you that. They shot pictures of everything and interviewed everybody who was in the battle reenactment. Trampled all over the place. Made Chief Tunney pretty mad."

Stanley could imagine. He didn't know much about police work, but he was learning, and he knew that Marilyn would be upset about anyone who messed up the crime scene. It wouldn't matter at all to her that they were the crew of a national television show.

"She told them about it, I'll bet," he said.

"She sure did. But it didn't do any good. There were twenty or thirty of them and only one of her."

The car drove out of the city and into the country. It was a beautiful day, and if there had been fog earlier, it had all burned away. The sky was a deep, pure blue, with only a few puffy cumulus clouds floating around in it. Pines lined the road, and Stanley relaxed a little. He had lived in cities most of his life, but he truly preferred the country and small towns like Higgins.

"Didn't Marilyn have any help?" he asked.

Bill grinned. "If you could call it that."

Stanley settled back in the seat. He had a feeling he knew what Bill was getting at.

"Officer Kunkel was on duty," Stanley said.

"You got it. Just as full of himself as ever, and doing the same bang-up job."

Stanley and Officer Kunkel didn't exactly get along. Kunkel was the kind of man who enjoyed his uniform just a little too much. It added a swagger to his walk and gave a mean edge to his voice. He had arrested Stanley once for breaking and entering and had even put Stanley in handcuffs. It would have given Kunkel great pleasure if Stanley had been sent to prison to be violated by sex offenders for several years if not for the rest of his natural life, but unfortunately for Kunkel's plans, Stanley hadn't been guilty. That incident hadn't improved his relationship with Kunkel at all.

"He made a lot of friends, I guess," Stanley said.

"Oh, you bet. They thought he was the proper stuff. They all want him to come to New York and be on TV with them."

Stanley smiled. The thought of Grant Tyler being pushed around a little by Officer Kunkel gave him a warm feeling inside.

"Has Marilyn found out anything?" he asked. "I mean, it must have been an accident, but does she know how it could have happened?"

"I don't think so. But then she doesn't tell me things like that. I'm not quite as well acquainted with her as some people I know."

Stanley didn't have anything to say to that. He could feel himself blushing, so he looked out the window and kept quiet.

When they got back to Blue Skies, Stanley stayed outside for a few minutes to check on the grounds. The tents were all gone, and all the trash had been cleaned up. The grass was mashed down and trampled a little, but otherwise there was hardly any sign of the previous day's events.

Unless you counted the yellow plastic crime-scene tape that seemed to be nearly everywhere.

Stanley looked out toward the little hill where the Union troops had been. There wasn't much cover there, but at the top there were plenty of trees and bushes where someone could have hidden. However, since he didn't even know whether he'd been shot from the front or the rear, it wouldn't do much good to speculate about hiding places.

For that matter it was possible that he'd been shot by someone who wasn't trying to hide: one of the Higgins citizens who'd circled around behind the Union men, for instance.

Not far from the hill was the place where the bandstand had been set up several months earlier for the grand opening of Blue Skies. A bluegrass group named Little Melvin and the Pacers had been on the stand playing a fiery version of "Rocky Top" when Belinda Grimsby had taken her dive into the salsa that day.

Stanley was beginning to think that having special events at his inn might not be such a good idea. He was getting plenty of publicity, all right, but it wasn't the kind he'd been hoping for. Maybe he was jinxed.

Stanley walked around to the back of the inn to see if the cats were around. Binky was there, lying in the sun and looking like a fully inflated gray football.

"Maybe you need to go on a diet, Binky," Stanley said.

Binky ignored him completely, but Sheba walked up and arched her back against his leg.

"I know what you're saying, Sheba. You're saying that you're glad to see me."

"Moeowrr," Sheba said.

"Either that, or you're hungry. Did Bill feed you this morning?"

"Moeowrr."

"Good. I knew he wouldn't forget. Is Cosmo around?"

"Moeowrr."

"Well, if you see him, tell him I'm glad to be back."

This time Sheba didn't respond. She walked over to Binky, licked him on the head a few times, then lay down as close to him as she could get.

Stanley watched them for a few seconds, wishing he could be as content as they seemed to be, and then he went inside to see if any of the day's guests had arrived. None had, but the smell of fried chicken was in the air.

Stanley wandered into the kitchen, where Caroline was standing at the stove. Cooking oil hissed and popped as she dropped pieces of chicken into the pan.

Stanley's mouth watered. The Colonel might have his special recipe with its secret herbs and spices, but his chicken wasn't a patch on Caroline's.

"Welcome back," Caroline said. "We'll be having that squash casserole you like, too. And mashed potatoes, cream gravy, and biscuits. Your favorites."

"Everything you cook is my favorite," Stanley said truthfully. "What about dessert?"

"Chocolate pie. It's cooling now."

Stanley looked over at the cabinet where the pie sat on a rack. The meringue looked light, fluffy, and perfect.

"How long?" he asked, trying not to think about the number of calories and fat grams he was soon going to ingest.

"Not long. We're going to have a guest, too."

"Who?"

"The police chief. I think she wants to talk to you."

"I'll bet she does," Stanley said.

⌒ 8 ⌒

Murder for Lunch

Stanley had known Marilyn Tunney since they had started elementary school together. She had been in his first-grade class, and they had been in the same homeroom for the next twelve years, right up until graduation.

Stanley had always been attracted to Marilyn, but even when they'd been dating, Stanley had been pretty sure he was much more serious about the relationship than Marilyn, and the romance had ended with their graduation, when Stanley's radio career took him away from Higgins.

Marilyn had stayed behind, married a local boy, and gone into police work mainly because that was her husband's interest. He had been the police chief before her but had suffered a heart attack on the job while performing a heroic rescue of a pet dog that had somehow gotten trapped in a storm drain. Marilyn, who had been a detective on the force, was promoted to replace him.

She and Stanley had kept in touch through the years. It had been easy enough for her to keep up with his career, especially after he had broken into network television, and Stanley, who loved high school reunions, always made it a point to spend some time with her whenever Higgins graduates got together.

He had never thought that they would be thrown closely together again. For one thing, he was happily married for many years to a wonderful wife, Jane, who had been as much responsible for his success as he had. Her death from breast cancer was the main reason that Stanley had retired from his TV work and moved back to Higgins. He wasn't interested in carrying on his career in the national limelight if Jane couldn't be there to share it with him.

Belinda Grimsby's murder had brought Marilyn and Stanley back into contact. Stanley had been interested in helping discover who had killed Belinda, and Marilyn was glad for his help. He had a knack for getting people to talk to him, and talking to people was a large part of any investigation. With a little luck, and after a few complications, Stanley had solved the case.

And now Marilyn was telling him about another murder that had occurred on the grounds of his inn. This one was different, however. It was a shooting, which was a lot less subtle than poisoning. Poisoners and shooters had to be different kinds of people, Stanley thought. They both got the same result, but the methods weren't at all alike.

"You were shot by someone at the top of the hill," Marilyn said. "So was Rance. We don't know yet whether the same gun was used. We don't have the equipment in Higgins to do the ballistics tests, so we sent the bullet elsewhere."

They were sitting at the kitchen table. Bill and Caroline had eaten with them, but Caroline had gone to her apartment when the meal was finished, and Bill was cleaning up, clattering the dishes behind them. The fried chicken was nothing but bones now, and the last of the gravy had been sopped up by the biscuits. A bit of chocolate pie was still left, but not much.

"Bullet?" Stanley said. "Wasn't there more than one?"

"That's one of the things we aren't certain about. We've found only one, but with all the stomping around out there, it's possible that we missed one. And there's always a chance that someone picked it up and didn't tell us."

Stanley thought about some of the TV people, but he wasn't sure any of them would do a thing like that. What reason would they have?

"How could one bullet have done so much damage?" he asked.

"It would have been easy. The bullet could have gone through the original target and hit you. It would have been slowed down a lot, but it would still have had enough force to knock you out."

Stanley felt slightly ill, and it had nothing to do with all the fried chicken he'd just eaten. It was bad enough to have been shot, but to think that the bullet had passed through someone else on its way to him was somehow even more offensive than the idea that he'd been shot in the first place. Calling Rance "the original target" didn't make things any better.

He tried to get his mind off the idea by asking, "How do you know I was shot from the top of the hill?"

"The angle of Rance's wound, for one thing. Also, we have to assume that you and Rance were both shot from the same place, or nearly the same place even if there was more than one bullet. He was shot in the head. The front of the head. It wasn't a pretty sight."

Stanley knew little about bullet wounds, and he didn't want to learn any more, not just at that moment.

"What kind of bullet did you find?" Stanley asked. "Was it a minié ball?"

"That's what it was. Now it looks more like a Milk Dud that someone stepped on. Anyone up on that hill could have fired it."

Stanley thought for a second about how a real battle must have been, with minié balls flying everywhere.

"You're lucky that it didn't take the top of your head right off," Marilyn said.

Stanley vaguely remembered what he'd been thinking as he lay on the grass. He didn't tell Marilyn, however. That business about the top of his head was another image that he didn't want to dwell on. His wound itched, and he resisted the urge to touch his stitches.

"Why would anyone want to shoot me and Rance?" he asked.

"That's a good question. I hope this doesn't hurt your feelings, Stanley, but I don't think anyone wanted to shoot you. I think that Rance was the target and that hitting you was just an accident, whether two minié balls were fired or whether it was just one."

Stanley was relieved. He didn't like the idea of being a target.

"Are you sure about that?"

Marilyn shook her head. "Of course not. I'm not sure about anything. I think you could see why if you wouldn't mind watching the whole thing on videotape. Your TV friends got some wonderful shots of the battle."

Stanley wasn't certain how he felt about watching the tape. Getting shot was bad enough. Having to see it happen all over again on video wasn't going to be pleasant.

But Marilyn clearly wanted him to watch, and he wasn't going to do anything to disappoint her if he could help it.

"All right," he said. "I'll watch the tape. We'll have to go in my room."

"Good idea," Bill said from the sink. "I was about to turn on the dishwasher. You're not going to be able to have much of a conversation in here."

Stanley stood up. "I'm ready."

"I'll get the tape," Marilyn said.

⟫ 9 ⟪

Pictures Never Lie

Stanley had a television set hidden in an armoire in his room. He seldom opened the armoire to watch the set. He wasn't much of a television watcher. He hadn't even turned on *Hello, World!* that morning in the hospital, although he'd been pretty sure his condition would be mentioned. But that he didn't often watch didn't mean that he wanted to be completely cut off from TV, so he kept the set in his room. It was just out of sight, not entirely out of mind.

He opened the armoire and turned the rocking chair to face it. Marilyn could have that seat, and he would sit at the desk.

He'd just gotten things ready when Marilyn came in. She had two videocassettes in her hand.

"Here it is. Are you sure you don't mind doing this?"

"I mind, all right, but I have to admit that I'm curious. I've seen tapes of myself doing the weather, and I've seen tapes of myself dressed in a clown outfit at supermarket openings. I've even seen a tape of myself in a dress. But I've never seen a tape of me getting shot."

Marilyn handed him a tape. "This will be a first for you then."

Stanley took the tape, walked over to the armoire, and inserted the tape into the VCR that sat on a shelf just below the TV set.

"You can have the rocking chair," he said.

Marilyn smiled as she sat down. "You're taking this better than I am."

"You mean watching me get shot is going to be hard on you, too?"

"It's always hard to watch something bad happen to someone you care about."

Stanley felt his head heating up. He wished he didn't blush so easily. It was foolish for a man his age to let something like that happen, he thought, but he couldn't help it. Some things you just couldn't do anything about.

He also couldn't think of any clever way to respond to Marilyn's remark. In fact, he couldn't think of any response at all, something that seemed to happen to him only when he was around Marilyn. So instead of talking, he turned on the TV set and the VCR and punched PLAY on the VCR's remote.

At first there was the usual blank screen filled with electrical "noise," but then the tape cleared. The first thing Stanley saw was the Union soldiers running down the hill.

"This isn't the only tape, is it?"

Marilyn said that it wasn't. "But it's the best one. It's not often that we get a shooting on tape."

"It should be a big help when it comes to finding out how Rance and I got shot."

"The operative word is *should*. It's not going to be much help at all, I'm afraid."

"Why not?"

"It's all your fault. Watch, and you'll see why."

Stanley watched and listened. Marilyn had been right. The tape was good. The cameraman had done such a good job that it was almost like watching an edited movie, and Len Wilson had been absolutely right about the mist and fog. They had given the whole thing an air of eerie authenticity so effective that even Stanley, who not only knew he was watching a tape but had been one of the actors in the drama, could almost believe that he was watching the real thing.

The rifles crashed, the smoke drifted into the mist and tree branches, the soldiers in their uniforms looked for all the world like men from another time. As Stanley watched, Rance emerged from the trees and gave his rebel yell, a sound so piercing that Stanley lowered the volume.

Stanley ran out of the trees right behind Rance, but Stanley's yell was so ineffective that it could hardly be heard, even though the rifles were quiet at that point.

"Now comes the bad part," Marilyn said. "In more ways than one."

The rifles were firing again, and Stanley almost didn't hear her. Then he saw Rance fall, and he saw himself falling, too, virtually at the same instant. It was difficult to tell which one of them had fallen first, which explained something that had been bothering Stanley. He couldn't remember seeing Rance fall that morning, and he'd been afraid that he might have suffered some kind of brain damage.

Now that he saw things on tape, Stanley realized that he could not have seen what happened to Rance. They had hit the ground almost simultaneously.

There was more to the tape than just Rance's fall, however. Stanley knew that if the tape was slowed down, it would show what had happened to Rance's head. Stanley didn't want to see that.

The cameraman wasn't interested in Rance. He focused on Stanley as he lay in the wet grass, not moving at all. He looked dead, very dead.

Watching himself, Stanley felt extremely uncomfortable, and his head started to throb as if the little man with the drum had moved back in.

"Right now that cameraman thinks you're doing a great acting job," Marilyn said.

"I wish I *had* been acting, but I wasn't."

"You know that. I know that. But the cameraman didn't know that. And since you're the star, he stayed with you for a while. And he'd been on you ever since you came out of the woods. You know what that means, don't you?"

Stanley had to admit that he didn't.

"It means that he wasn't taking any shots of the soldiers who were firing at you."

"And that's why you said this was the bad part?"

"I said it was bad in more ways than one. I really don't like seeing you fall, Stanley. It's just too real."

She reached over and touched Stanley's hand, and his temperature immediately shot up about two degrees.

"What about the other cameramen?" he asked. "I know there were at least two others."

Marilyn held up the other tape that she'd brought to the room.

"Oh."

"It's not much better," Marilyn said. "It shows the men on the hill, but it doesn't show you and Rance at the same time. We might be able to synchronize the tapes to figure out just which one of them might have been firing when you were shot, but it's going to be complicated. And then there's the possibility of stop-action and computer enhancement. The FBI lab has agreed to look at the tapes and see what can be done."

Stanley wasn't interested in labs. "How do you know it was one of the soldiers?"

"We don't know that it was. But they were up there. They were firing. One of them could have been using minié balls instead of just wadding. More than one of them could have been."

"There could have been someone else up there, too."

"Sure," Marilyn said. "But if there was, we won't ever be able to prove it. Too many other people were there after you were shot. If there was someone running around with an 1853 Enfield musket, he'd be pretty obvious."

"There were several people with muskets."

"But they were all in uniform. Anyone else would stand out a lot in that crowd."

Stanley knew that she was right. Considering how serious everyone was about reenacting, someone who wasn't part of the group couldn't slip by unnoticed.

"So Rance was shot by someone who was up on that hill," he said.

"It looks that way. We can't rule out the possibility that some-one could have hidden there, but we haven't found a hiding place yet."

Stanley thought it over. He didn't think there was any place someone could hide on the hill. There were a few trees, but not enough to offer much cover. The reenactors would have seen anyone who was there, and by now Marilyn would have ques-tioned all of them.

"Okay, then," he said. "We were shot by one of the reenac-tors. It must have been some kind of accident. No one would shoot Rance on purpose."

"Why not?"

Fair weather cometh out of the north.

—Job 37:22

Thunder is good, thunder is impressive;
but it is the lightning that does the work.

—Mark Twain

⬅ 10 ➡

No Amateurs Need Apply

Stanley was a little surprised by Marilyn's comment. He said, "Rance Wofford is a very respected businessman in Higgins. Or he was. Who'd want to kill him?"

"You want the names?" Marilyn asked.

"You have names?"

"Duffy Weeks, Neddy Drake, Al Walker, and Burl Cabot. They're the ones who circled around to the top of the hill. And then there's Lacy Falk."

"Lacy Falk? You're kidding."

"I'm not kidding. I wish I were."

"But you just told me that whoever killed Rance would have had to be carrying a rifle. I saw Lacy, and she wasn't carrying anything. And, uh . . ."

Stanley stopped and looked at the TV set, where the fighting was now all over. Everyone had realized what had happened, and people were gathering around his prostrate body. He supposed they were gathering around Rance's body, too, but the cameraman wasn't interested in how badly a local man might be hurt, not until the health and well-being of the former *Hello, World!* weatherman were determined.

"You can turn that off," Marilyn said. "We don't need to see the rest of it."

Stanley took the remote from his desk and stopped the VCR. Then he clicked off the television set.

"I know what you're thinking," Marilyn told him. "You're thinking that Lacy didn't have a rifle when you saw her."

"That's right."

"And that she didn't have any place to conceal one."

Stanley's head was warming up. Lacy couldn't have concealed a fountain pen in what she'd been wearing. "That's right, too."

"Don't worry, Stanley. We're not going to railroad her just because she was dressed in her shimmy-tail. But she was up on that hill for some reason. We're going to have to question her about it."

"And everyone else you named was up there, too?"

"That's right. All four of them. Five, counting Lacy, and she certainly counts. They're all on the tape."

"But those men have lived here all their lives. And Lacy's been here for years. They wouldn't kill Rance."

"You probably didn't think anyone would kill Belinda Grimsby, either."

"Of course not," Stanley said. "But that was different. That was—"

Marilyn got out of the rocker, walked to the armoire, and punched the EJECT button on the VCR. The tape popped partway out, and she removed it.

"Belinda wasn't any different. She's just as dead as Rance is. And it's highly likely that one of the men I named is Rance's killer. Now I have to find out which one had a motive."

Stanley said, "Maybe there wasn't a motive. The shooting must have been an accident. Surely someone made some kind of mistake and loaded a minié ball without realizing it."

"How much do you know about firing black-powder weapons, Stanley?"

Stanley had to admit that he didn't know much at all about any kind of weapons, much less black-powder rifles.

Marilyn enlightened him. "It's not a very complicated process, but it does take a while. And you have to load the minié ball very deliberately. It couldn't have been an accident, Stanley."

"You're sure?"

"I'm not one hundred percent certain, no. But I'm pretty sure. I'm sorry, Stanley."

"Damn." Stanley didn't use profanity often, but the expression was heartfelt. "What do we do now?"

"What do you mean, *we*?"

"You're going to let me help, aren't you? I mean, this is worse than the last time. Not only has someone been killed on my property, I've been shot, too. I have a right to find out who did it."

"No, you don't. You're a private citizen. I'm the one who has a right to find out who did it. In fact, it's my job. It's what the citizens of Higgins pay me for."

"But last time you said you wanted my help."

"You weren't shot last time. It's barely possible that someone was trying to kill you instead of Rance."

"I thought you'd already dismissed that idea."

"I didn't dismiss it. I just said that it wasn't likely. But it's certainly possible."

Stanley didn't like to think about that angle. And he didn't agree with Marilyn. He didn't think it was possible that any of the men she'd named would want to kill him. He knew them all, but only slightly. They had no arguments with him and no reason to want him dead.

"Have you already started questioning people?" he asked.

"Yes. We've interviewed a few of them. And we'll be talking to a lot of others. But you don't need to concern yourself with it. It's police business."

"Belinda was police business, too."

"That's true, and I have to admit that you were a big help with that case. But this time I think it would be for the best if you didn't get involved."

Stanley thought of himself as an even-tempered person, someone who rarely got angry. And of all the people he didn't want to get angry with, Marilyn was right there at the top of the list.

Still, he didn't like the idea that he was being left out of the investigation. He thought he'd proved himself useful in the Belinda Grimsby situation. In fact, he'd solved the case. Not that Marilyn couldn't have done it without him, but Stanley had enjoyed trying to ferret out information by talking to people and analyzing their possible motives. To tell the truth, he'd even liked being a little sneaky, sort of like Jim Rockford only slightly heftier. And with a little less hair. Okay, with a lot less hair, but what difference did hair make, anyhow? It didn't make you a better investigator. Stanley was sure of that.

"I want to be involved," he said. "It's only fair."

"Fair doesn't have anything to do with it. I've already assigned an investigator, and I don't want you getting in his way."

"Not Officer Kunkel, I hope."

Marilyn had to smile at that. "No. Not him. Brad Bridger."

"I see. I'm sure he'll be much better than Officer Kunkel or me."

Brad Bridger was one of two detectives on the Higgins police force. He was a couple of years younger than Stanley and recently divorced. He was tall and lean, and he had more hair than Jim Rockford. Stanley had met him only casually, but he seemed likable enough.

"He's a professional," Marilyn said. "This isn't a job for amateurs."

Stanley couldn't argue with that. Except to say that he'd done pretty well for an amateur once before.

"Yes, but you nearly got yourself killed," Marilyn said.

"But I didn't."

"Are we having a fight here?"

"I don't think so," Stanley said. "Just a mild difference of opinion."

"Let's hope it doesn't go beyond mild. I have to get back to the station now, and I'll let you know as soon as we find anything solid."

Stanley felt as if he'd been dismissed. And in his own bedroom, to boot. Well, there wasn't much he could do about it.

"Just how busy are you going to be?" he asked.

"Very busy, but don't worry. I'll call you."

"Great," Stanley said, trying to put some semblance of enthusiasm in his voice. It wasn't easy, and he didn't think he succeeded. "I'm sure you'll have someone behind bars in mere hours."

"It might take a little longer."

"I was afraid you'd tell me that."

≈ 11 ≈

The Green-Eyed Monster

Stanley had been instructed not to do any heavy work, but shortly after Marilyn left, he went out behind the inn to turn the compost pile. He needed to do something to take his mind off what had just happened, and messing around with compost was just the thing.

Or so he thought until he got started. There were some unique smells to distract him, all right, and he worked up a sweat before many minutes had passed, but he couldn't stop thinking about Marilyn and the way she'd acted.

True, she'd seemed genuinely concerned about him, and she'd also seemed upset by what had happened. But as soon as he'd suggested that he might want to help her out, she'd become distant and a little cold. Or so it appeared to Stanley.

And then there was Brad Bridger. It was bad enough that he was fairly good-looking and had a name like some character on *The Bold and the Beautiful*. It was even worse that Stanley thought he'd detected a touch too much warmth in Marilyn's tone when she'd mentioned his name.

Stanley forked over a heap of compost, releasing the rich odor of coffee grounds mixed with orange peel and something that was even more powerful than either but which Stanley couldn't identify.

"Am I getting jealous?" he asked himself.

"You're damned right," he answered.

Then he remembered hearing somewhere that talking to yourself wasn't a bad sign but that answering yourself was. Maybe he'd been out in the sun too long. A man with a mild concussion couldn't afford to take chances.

He went back into the inn and cleaned up just in time to welcome the first of his night's guests, the Skidmores, a man and woman about Stanley's age. Mr. Skidmore told him in an unmistakable Texas accent that they were on their honeymoon. Stanley was glad to know that a pair of middle-aged married people could look so happy. He thought about Marilyn again, but he pushed the thought away.

"And we just love what we've seen of Virginia," Mrs. Skidmore said. "It's almost as pretty as Texas."

She didn't sound at all like her husband. Stanley would have bet money she was from the Midwest, Chicago, maybe. But she was being loyal to her husband's home state, which Stanley thought was nice.

Stanley had been to Texas more than once, but he didn't think it would be necessary for him to express his opinion of its beauty. He said, "I'm glad you like it here, and I hope you'll enjoy your stay in Blue Skies."

"I'm sure we will," Mr. Skidmore said, looking at Stanley's stitches. "We saw you on TV the other day, and we were so glad to hear that you weren't seriously hurt. That was a terrible accident. How's your head?"

"It's fine, thanks. Let me show you to your room."

He led them upstairs to the Washington Room. Although no signs indicated that the rooms had names, Stanley had put a portrait of a Virginia-born president in each one. There were five rooms, and the pictures were of Washington, Jefferson, Madison, Monroe, and Wilson, which of course meant that Stanley could add three more rooms to his inn and still have presidents to name them for if he wanted to do so. Virginia wasn't called "the mother of presidents" for nothing.

Stanley didn't have any plans for expansion just yet, however, so Tyler, Taylor, and Harrison would just have to go without having rooms named for them in Blue Skies. Stanley didn't think they'd mind.

The Skidmores liked their room, and Stanley was flattered when Mrs. Skidmore, who had asked him to call her Sheila, remarked on the handmade quilt that covered the bed.

"I'll bet it's a hundred years old," she said.

It wasn't, and Stanley admitted it. He'd bought it at an antique store, but it had been made by a women's church group in Higgins. It had cost almost as much as many genuine antiques, however.

The room also had period furniture and a washbasin and pitcher on a washstand.

"I hope we're not going to have to bathe in here," Sheila said.

"Don't worry," Stanley told her. "We have indoor plumbing, and hot water, too."

He showed them the bathroom and decided not to mention the chamber pot that was under their bed. Stanley liked to have something special in each bedroom, and the chamber pot was it for the Washington Room. The Jefferson Room had a canopy bed, while the Madison Room had a parquet floor. The Monroe Room had a marble-topped dresser and nightstand that Hal Tipton had moved in there after Stanley had decided to move the Franklin stove to the Wilson Room, the only room without a fireplace.

"And are we right that you serve supper as well as breakfast if we want it?" Sheila asked.

"That's right," Stanley said. "The best supper in the state of Virginia. All you have to do is ask in advance. There'll be a charge added to your bill, of course."

Sheila looked at her husband, who nodded his assent. "Well, sign us up," she said.

Stanley waited until the rest of his guests were checked in, including couples from Louisiana, Nebraska, New York, and Massachusetts. Each time, someone asked about his wound. He'd always known that *Hello, World!* had a wide audience, but he was beginning to believe that there was no one in America who didn't watch.

After he'd settled everyone into the upstairs rooms, he went into the kitchen, where Caroline Caldwell was getting ready to begin cooking dinner.

"Two couples for dinner. All the others are going into Alexandria." He paused. "They don't know what they're missing."

"They'll find out at breakfast," Caroline said, and Stanley gave her a hard look. He thought she might actually have made a little joke. If she had, it would be a first.

"I'll be here, too," he said. "But I'll be out for the rest of the afternoon. If the guests need anything, can Bill take care of them?"

"Long as they don't fall in the creek. Where are you going to be if we need you?"

"I'll be at the nursing home."

There was only one nursing home in Higgins. It was called Wooded Acres, which made it sound like an exclusive housing addition. But it was a nursing home, all right.

"It's about time you paid a visit to your uncle," Caroline said.

"No need trying to make me feel guilty. I go as often as I can."

And he did. Stanley's uncle Martin had been in the nursing home for the last three years, since before Stanley had moved back to Higgins. Stanley had visited him fairly regularly, but at times he was just too busy. Like when he was investigating a murder.

"You wait a minute," Caroline said. "I want to send him a piece of pie that was left over from lunch."

The pie was sitting on the stove. A mesh cover protected it from the cats, all of whom were almost as fond of chocolate pie as Stanley was. Sheba didn't like the filling, however. She preferred the crust.

Caroline removed the cover and cut a generous slice of pie. She put it on a paper plate that she had taken from one of the cabinets and covered it with plastic wrap.

"You be careful not to let that wrap touch the meringue,"

she told Stanley. "Meringue sticks to plastic and it'll mess up the looks of the pie."

Stanley said that he'd be careful.

"What was it that made you decide to go see Mr. Waters this afternoon?" Caroline asked as he was leaving.

"I'm going to ask him about the war," Stanley said, knowing that he didn't have to identify which war he meant.

"He can tell you as much as anybody. Don't forget that pie, now."

Stanley picked it up.

"Don't you go and eat it, now. That's for Mr. Waters."

"I'll be good," Stanley promised.

"That'll be the day."

❧ 12 ❧

Checker Lesson

The drive out to Wooded Acres didn't take long. The nursing home was located on the north side of town, out past the jail and the high school. When Stanley thought about it, which wasn't often, it struck him as oddly appropriate that the three institutions were in such close proximity.

Stanley drove into the parking lot and found a place beside a white van with WOODED ACRES painted on the side. He got out of the car and looked around. Tall pine trees shaded the building, and the grass was neatly trimmed. Several people sat motionless in wheelchairs on the porch, their hands clutching the blankets that were pulled up on their laps. A man and a woman shuffled along side by side behind their walkers.

Stanley recognized the couple as Annie and Blaine Minton. They were brother and sister. Annie had been Stanley's high school algebra teacher.

"Hello, Miss Minton," he said, walking up to stand near her.

Miss Minton looked at him with watery blue eyes. "Is that you, Stanley Waters?"

"Yes, ma'am. How are you today?"

"How do I look?"

Her hair was wispy and white, her face was mostly wrinkles, and her hands looked like a bird's claws.

"You look just fine, Miss Minton," Stanley said.

Miss Minton smiled and shook her head sadly. "You always did have a line of bull about a mile long, Stanley. Isn't that right, Blaine?"

Blaine didn't say a word. He just stared off into the distance as if there were something there that only he could see and understand.

"Blaine's not exactly on top of his game these days," Miss Minton said. "Most of the time, anyway. What brings you out here, Stanley? Want to brush up on the quadratic equation?"

Stanley hated to admit it, but he had no idea what the quadratic equation was.

"I'm not surprised," Miss Minton said. "Sometimes I think I just wasted all those years of teaching. Probably not a single student I ever had remembers the quadratic equation."

"Ungrateful turds," Blaine said. His voice sounded a little like a crow cawing.

"You'll have to excuse Blaine's language," Miss Minton said. "Sometimes he's a bit plainspoken."

"Sometimes I am, too," Stanley said.

"I don't remember that about you. You were always very polite and well behaved in class. Not like some I could name. What brings you out here, anyway?"

"I came to see Uncle Martin."

"I was pretty sure that pie wasn't for me. Well, Martin's right inside, probably playing checkers with Goob Henry, as usual. Don't let us keep you."

"It was good to see you, Miss Minton. You, too, Mr. Minton."

Blaine stared up at the blue sky, and Stanley turned to go.

"$ax^2 + bx + c = 0$," Blaine said to his back.

Stanley turned around and looked at him. He was staring off at the sky again.

"That's the quadratic equation," Miss Minton explained. "Just in case you were wondering."

"I had a feeling that's what it was," Stanley said.

Miss Minton smiled. "Blaine might be a little slow in some ways, but he still knows his math."

"Thank you, Mr. Minton," Stanley said.

"Which is more than I can say for some people," Miss Minton went on as if Stanley hadn't spoken. She looked at him as if to say that he knew whom she meant.

"I'm sure it'll come in handy someday," Stanley said. "Thanks again, Mr. Minton."

Blaine didn't respond, and Stanley went inside. The first thing that always struck him about Wooded Acres was how noisy it was. The communal TV set in the parlor was turned up loud, and Alex Trebek was asking the contestants on *Jeopardy!* to make their final wagers based on the fact that the category was "U.S. presidents."

Several people sitting in front of the set were talking at the top of their voices about something that seemed to have nothing at all to do with the game show. Stanley thought he heard the words "goddamned liberal Democrats," but he might have been wrong.

Off down one of the hallways, someone was screaming. It wasn't a scream of pain. It was just a scream. No one was paying it any attention, not even the nurse at the desk. She was reading an issue of *Cosmopolitan* as if she were sitting all alone in a room at home.

Stanley went over to the game table where two old men sat and stared down at a checkerboard covered with bottle caps. Half the caps were right-side up; the other half were upside down.

Goob Henry was eighty-six years old. He weighed around a hundred pounds and seemed to shrink into his clothes. His shirt collar was at least three sizes too large, and his skin hung on him as loosely as the shirt.

Stanley's uncle Martin was the same age as Goob, but more than twice Goob's size. He was even balder than Stanley, and he wore a pair of Dickies overalls over a white shirt. The legs of the overalls were too long and flopped down over a pair of worn leather house shoes.

Stanley said, "Hey, Uncle Martin, what's going on?"

"I'm about to give Goob his checker lesson for the day," Uncle Martin said out of one side of his mouth. He'd had a stroke that paralyzed his right side. "The lesson starts just as soon as we hear the final *Jeopardy!* answer. You be quiet now, so we can listen."

Stanley didn't see how they could hear above all the other noise, but he supposed they were used to it. He stood quietly through what seemed like about eighteen commercials. Finally Alex Trebek returned and read the answer:

"He was the first vice president to succeed to the presidency upon the death of an incumbent."

The *Jeopardy!* theme began to play as the contestants wrote their answers, being sure, Stanley hoped, to put them in the form of a question.

"Must be kiddie week," Uncle Martin said. "Any damn fool off the street knows that one."

"I can even tell you what *county* he was born in," Goob said. "How about you, Stanley?"

Stanley didn't have a broad knowledge of American history, but when it came to presidents who'd been born in Virginia, it was hard to fool him.

"Charles City County," he said.

"Well, by golly," Goob said. "There might be some hope for the younger generation after all."

Stanley stood up a little straighter. It had been a long time since someone had spoken of him as part of the younger generation. Even if it wasn't true, it made him feel good.

"You didn't say what his name was, though," Uncle Martin announced.

"John Tyler," Stanley told him.

"Right you are. Now let's see if any of those idiots on TV get it right."

The first contestant's answer (or question, if you wanted to look at it that way) was Harry Truman.

Goob Henry groaned. "Morons. The whole world is full of morons."

The second contestant guessed William Henry Harrison,

who, as Stanley well knew, was the president that John Tyler had succeeded.

"You have to give her credit for coming close," Goob said. "Old Tippecanoe. All right, Stanley, where was he born?"

"That's another easy one," Stanley said. "Charles City County."

"Right you are," Uncle Martin said. "Two Charles City County boys in the White House, one right after the other."

The third contestant had written "John Tyler," and when Trebek congratulated her for being the winner, Uncle Martin and Goob lost interest in the program.

"One thing they could've asked," Goob said, "was which presidents they were. You're pretty sharp today, Stanley. Think you know?"

Stanley thought he knew. "Ninth and tenth."

Goob gave out with a cackley laugh. "You wasted your time being a weatherman, boy. You should've been a history professor at some university."

"Don't let him fool you," Uncle Martin said. "If you threw out the Virginia presidents, he'd be lost."

"That's right," Stanley agreed, looking around for a chair. "How are things going out here these days?"

"Not too bad," Uncle Martin said. "There's a chair over there by Thelma Lenz, if you don't mind a wheelchair."

"I don't mind."

"Go get it then. You can set that pie down here on the table if it's for me. Goob and I can eat it later."

Stanley set the pie on the table and got the chair. By the time he'd rolled it over to the table and sat down, the checker game was in progress. Stanley knew better than to interrupt. He sat quietly and watched as Goob set a trap that led to his jumping three of Uncle Martin's bottle caps at once and getting a king in the bargain.

"King me," Goob said, cackling. "I guess Stanley can see who's getting the checker lesson today, and it's not me."

The game didn't take long after that. Uncle Martin was never able to recover from Goob's first maneuver, and Goob won easily.

"Want another game?" Goob asked. "I'll give you a chance to get your pride back."

"Maybe later," Uncle Martin said. "Right now, I guess we should find out why Stanley came to visit."

"I came to see you and bring you some pie," Stanley said. "That's a good reason, isn't it?"

"Sure is, but that's not all there is to it. I can see you're a little antsy about something, so you might as well tell me what it is. Unless it's private. If it is, you can just give Goob's wheelchair a shove and send him over there to watch *Oprah* with everybody else. Maybe he'll sign up for her book club."

"I don't want to watch *Oprah*," Goob said. "And I don't want to sign up for any book club. My eyes are too bad for reading. Besides, if there's something to hear, I want to hear it."

Stanley didn't mind talking in front of Goob. In fact, he thought that Goob might have something to contribute to the conversation.

"I want to talk to you about a murder," Stanley said.

"Sounds good," Uncle Martin said. "Who're we gonna kill?"

⤠ 13 ⤟

The Case of the Missing Candy Bars

"That's not exactly what I had in mind," Stanley said.

"Too bad," Goob said. "I'd like to kill the son of a bitch who's been stealing my Snickers bars."

"Has someone been taking them again?" Stanley asked.

Goob shot a significant look at Uncle Martin. "*Someone* has, all right. I don't know who it is, because I can't catch him at it."

"Him or *her*," Uncle Martin said.

"Fine. Him or *her*. But whoever it is, capital punishment is too good for him. Or her."

Uncle Martin and Goob were roommates. Both men, though somewhat physically impaired, were in firm possession of all their mental faculties, and most of the time they got along just fine. But every now and then there was a little tension.

Usually it concerned Goob's Snickers bars, which had a way of disappearing, at least according to Goob. Uncle Martin professed to have no knowledge of them.

"I hope you aren't looking at me," Uncle Martin said. "I never took a one of your Snickers. I don't even know where you're hiding them now."

"And I'm not going to tell you, either. If I did, they'd probably disappear twice as fast."

Stanley thought it was time to change the subject. "We've got some of Caroline's chocolate pie here. It's better than any Snickers ever thought about being. Why don't I go get some plates and you two can have a slice."

Goob eyed the pie. "Caroline does make a fine pie, and I'd admire to have a slice of it. But that doesn't mean I'm in a mood to forget about the Snickers bars."

"Maybe you could get your friend the police chief to come out here and run an investigation," Uncle Martin told Stanley. " 'The Case of the Missing Candy Bars.' "

"It's not funny," Goob said.

"I'll go get the plates," Stanley told them. "And you two can calm down."

He went into the dining area and got two dessert plates, a knife, and two forks from one of the women who were working back in the kitchen. He picked up some paper napkins from one of the tables and returned to the other room, where Goob and Uncle Martin were talking about Rance Wofford.

Stanley overheard them. "You knew all along what I was here for," he said as he sliced the pie.

"We watch a lot of TV," Uncle Martin said, accepting the plate that Stanley handed him. "We know all about Rance Wofford and you getting shot. We were just having a little fun."

"That's right," Goob said, taking his own plate. "We old guys have to get our laughs any way we can. How's that head of yours? Looks like the doctor did a good job on the stitches."

"The head's fine. Doesn't hurt a bit. Well, not much. They gave me some pills to take if the pain got too bad. So far it hasn't."

Uncle Martin forked a bite of pie into his mouth and chewed it. When he was finished, he said, "You can tell Caroline she hasn't lost her touch."

"She'll be glad to hear it," Stanley said. "Now, what can you tell me about Rance Wofford?"

"We can tell you plenty," Goob said. "We hear a lot of things in this place."

Goob was telling the simple truth. He and Uncle Martin watched a lot of TV, true, and they played checkers nearly every day, but the main occupation in the nursing home was gossiping. Everyone who came to visit a friend or relative had to have something to talk about, and generally the talk ran to the things that were going on in town—the spicier the better. Anything particularly interesting was repeated to everyone in the home within fifteen minutes.

Stanley said, "I haven't been back in Higgins very long, and Rance didn't live here when I left. So I don't know much about him at all. I want to know the gossip. I want to know why someone might want to kill him."

"He's got more money than God," Goob said. "Or he did have. You can start right there. I never knew of a rich man who didn't have plenty of enemies."

"There's nothing wrong with having money," Stanley protested.

"You can say that because you've got so much of it," Uncle Martin said. "Help me out with the napkin, Stanley."

Stanley wiped pie crumbs from the corner of Uncle Martin's mouth.

"Thanks," Uncle Martin said. "No offense, Stanley, but you're not going about this the right way. You shouldn't be defending Wofford. You should be thinking about his insurance policy and his beneficiaries."

"Oh. Right. Follow the money."

Goob nodded. "Always a good idea. Should you be writing this down, Stanley? We don't want you to forget anything."

"I'll remember," Stanley said, hoping he wasn't lying. "Insurance. See? I got it."

"Another thing," Uncle Martin said. "Did you know that Wofford owned the building that Bushwhackers is in?"

Stanley said that he hadn't known that.

"Well, he does. He bought up a lot of places when he moved here about ten years ago. Claimed he'd made plenty of money in real estate in D.C., but he was tired of the big city. So he came here and started in to make more money. That Bushwhackers business is owned by a woman named Lacy Falk."

"I know Lacy," Stanley said. "She cuts my hair."

"Now there's a rough job," Goob said, eyeing the fringe of

hair that grew around the sides and back of Stanley's head. "I'll bet it takes her all day."

Stanley smiled. He was used to bald jokes.

"As I was saying," Uncle Martin continued, "Miss Falk owns Bushwhackers. She's a nice woman, comes out here to cut people's hair for free."

"Those who need it, that is," Goob added.

"Never mind him," Uncle Martin said. "He's jealous because women find us bald men more attractive than old farts with combovers."

"Bull corn," Goob said, patting the thin locks that he'd smoothed across his bald spot.

"About Lacy Falk," Stanley said.

"She said something not long ago," Uncle Martin told him. "It might not mean anything, but she told me and Goob that Wofford was going to raise her rent so much that she might lose the shop. She thinks he wanted her to move out so he could put in a fancy restaurant."

"Why didn't he just refuse to renew her lease?" Stanley asked.

"Something in the contract," Uncle Martin said. "She got first chance at the building when the lease ran out."

"I think he put the moves on her, too," Goob said. "He's a real ladies' man, they say."

Stanley seemed to recall having heard that Wofford had an unusually high opinion of his good looks and his aptitude with women.

"For that matter, *you* might have had a reason to kill him, Stanley," Uncle Martin said. "We hear he's got that hotel he bought all fixed up. He might cut you out of some business."

Stanley didn't think that was likely. People who stayed in a hotel weren't interested in the services of his inn, and vice versa.

"What about Burl Cabot?" he asked.

Goob and Uncle Martin glanced at one another, then looked back at Stanley.

"You know his mother's in here?" Uncle Martin said.

Stanley hadn't known.

"She's a fine woman. He's real good about visiting her, and we wouldn't want anything we said to get back to her."

Stanley understood. "I can keep a secret."

"Well, then, there's been talk that Burl's wife was running around with Rance. Burl does okay with those auto parts of his, but he's not anywhere near as rich as Rance Wofford was. Money can turn a woman's head."

Burl Cabot seemed to Stanley like the kind of man who'd want to use his physical strength, not an impersonal thing like a rifle, to get revenge on someone who was fooling around with his wife, but Stanley filed the information away in his head.

Uncle Martin pushed his plate away, and Stanley helped him wipe his mouth. Goob was finished, too, but he continued to pick at the crumbs of crust that remained.

"Do you know anything about Neddy Drake?" Stanley asked.

"Everybody knows about him," Goob said. "The Martians took out his liver and put in some kind of space gadget."

"It wasn't Martians," Uncle Martin said. "It was just space-men. And it wasn't his liver. It was his pancreas. Or his prostate. Or maybe his pyloric valve. Started with a *p*, anyhow."

Goob didn't argue. "Anybody crazy enough to think he's been carried off in a flying saucer by little green men might do nearly anything."

"They were white," Uncle Martin said. "Little *white* men. White as ghosts."

"Never mind," Stanley said. "Color doesn't matter. Did Neddy have any connection with Rance Wofford?"

"Sure he did," Uncle Martin said. "He owns that little building where his fried chicken business is. Wofford was going to buy him out and lease the building to some franchise place. Neddy turned him down."

"But Wofford doesn't take no for an answer," Goob said. "Not if he can help it. I hear that health-food store across the street from Neddy's place isn't doing too well. Wofford might buy it and put a franchise in there just to run Neddy out of business."

Stanley thought that Rance Wofford was beginning to sound like a real jerk.

"How about Al Walker?" he asked.

"Al's a nice enough man," Goob said. "He teaches math. I don't think a math teacher would shoot anybody, do you?"

Uncle Martin didn't think so either. "He might poison them, though. That's more like what a teacher would do."

Stanley didn't want to talk about poison. He'd already had one bad experience with poison, and that was enough.

He asked, "Did he know Rance?"

Uncle Martin and Goob didn't know of any connection between the two men, so Stanley moved on to Duffy Weeks.

"I knew him back when he was just plain Harold," Goob said. "I used to stop by Duffy's Tavern now and then for a beer, like a lot of folks did. I think Wofford owned that building, too."

"He did," Uncle Martin said. "He might've been trying to push Duffy out like he was Lacy, and like he wanted to do with Neddy. Something was bothering Duffy, that's for sure. He's taken to drinking way too much."

Stanley had heard that rumor already. "That's all you know?"

"It's more than you knew when you came in here," Uncle Martin said.

"I wasn't criticizing," Stanley said. "I just wondered if there was anything else you could tell me."

"Can't think of a thing," Goob said. "But you come back real soon with some more pie and we might have something for you."

Stanley gathered up the plates, forks, napkins, and the knife. "I'll just take these back to the kitchen. While I'm gone, see if you can remember anything else."

He left the two old men at the table arguing over whether Neddy Drake's spacemen were green or white and just what part of Neddy's body had been replaced by the interstellar prosthesis.

Stanley was sure they'd still be arguing when he returned. A good argument was almost as good as gossip, and though Stanley hated to admit it, it was a lot better than whatever might be on TV.

Stanley came back to the table with two cups of steaming black coffee.

"Now that's exactly what I was hoping you'd bring with you," Goob said. "I'm gonna saucer and blow mine, if you don't mind."

Stanley said that he didn't mind.

"Bad manners, if you ask me," Uncle Martin said.

"Nobody asked you," Goob said, pouring some coffee into his saucer. He blew on it several times, then picked up the saucer and tipped it to his mouth.

"Only way to drink hot coffee," he said after he'd swallowed.

Uncle Martin shook his head disgustedly and sipped noisily from his cup.

"What did you two think of the reenactment on TV?" Stanley asked. "Forgetting that Rance got shot, I mean. How did it look?"

"Looked real enough, I guess," Uncle Martin said. "Nice and spooky in the mist and all."

Stanley wondered what the two old men thought about the Civil War. They were old enough to have been around when plenty of veterans of that conflict had been alive and sitting around the Higgins courthouse square. Now there was only a statue there.

Some people objected to the statue's presence, but Stanley wasn't one of them. He didn't find such a memorial offensive at all, even though his own ancestors had been on the losing side of the conflict. To him, the statue resembled nothing so much as a tired human being, a man who had done what he believed to be his duty but who was now fed up with the war and the fighting and who wanted nothing more than to find his way back home.

Goob and Uncle Martin were also old enough to have grown up at a time when memories of "the Woah" were still bitter and when people in the South still thought that the only good Yankee was a dead one.

"Do you ever think about the war?" Stanley asked.

Uncle Martin took a sip of coffee and looked off into the distance. After a few seconds he said, "Not anymore."

"I used to," Goob said. "When I was a youngster. But I'm like Martin. I never think of it now. It was all over with a long time ago, and it probably turned out the way it should have."

"The South was right about some things," Uncle Martin said. "It was right about how important things like duty and responsibility are. But it was wrong about the slaves. I think a lot of people knew that, even then. They were just too stubborn to back down."

"Lot of people are still like that," Goob said, looking at Uncle Martin. "Stubborn, that is."

"Never mind," Stanley said. "I have to get back to the inn for dinner. You two keep all this confidential, all right?"

Goob and Uncle Martin said they would, and Stanley turned to go. Before he reached the door, however, Uncle Martin called him back.

"We did forget something," Uncle Martin said. "I just remembered Al Walker might be a teacher and a nice guy, but he's pretty good with black powder."

"I heard about that," Stanley said.

"Well, whoever shot Rance would have to be good," Uncle Martin said. "Those old rifles aren't exactly models of accuracy."

"Yeah," Goob said. "You're lucky whoever shot Rance didn't miss him completely and blow your head off instead."

"You two are a real comfort," Stanley said.

⌐ 14 ⌐

The Pause
That Refreshes

Stanley drove back to the inn in a thoughtful frame of mind. It appeared that everyone in a position to shoot Rance Wofford had a good reason to do so, except for Al Walker, and Walker couldn't be entirely discounted. There might be something that Stanley hadn't found out about yet, and Walker was reputedly the best shot of the whole bunch.

If Agatha Christie had been in charge of things, Al Walker would likely be the guilty party. He had the necessary skill, he had the opportunity, and he was the least likely suspect.

Well, Stanley thought with a smile, now that I've solved the crime, all I have to do is provide a motive, and Al Walker is as good as convicted.

When he got to town, Stanley decided to go by M & B Antiques. It was getting late in the afternoon, but Stanley was sure the store would still be open.

It was. Stanley parked and went inside.

Tommy Bright, Barry Miller's partner, had a cloth in his hand and was buffing an old Coca-Cola dispenser that sat on a table. The dispenser was bright red with white lettering, and it had a rounded top.

"Hi, Stanley," Tommy said, slapping the cloth against the table.

Tommy wore a pair of white Reebok walking shoes, ice blue jeans, and a navy blue blazer. He was short and dapper and drove a 1957 Chevy two-door hardtop that Stanley greatly admired. The car was almost the same colors as the Coke machine.

"See that?" Tommy said, pointing to the price painted in white on the dispenser. "Five cents a bottle. Put in your nickel, push down on this handle"—he gave the handle a little rattle—"and out comes a Co'-Cola in a six-ounce, green glass bottle."

"The ones in the little bottle were the best-tasting Cokes they ever made," Stanley said.

"Right you are. They can say what they want, but all that air in those big plastic bottles does something to the flavor. And a can? Well, honestly, what can I say."

"You don't have to say a thing. I know what you mean."

"A man with your taste and perception really should have a machine like this," Tommy said. "It would look great at the inn. You could put it in the parlor or maybe in a hallway. It would give the guests a kick to buy a Coke for a nickel."

Stanley was tempted. The machine looked almost new, and it would add a nice nostalgic touch to the inn.

"Does it work?"

Tommy looked at Stanley incredulously and put the hand holding the rag to his heart. "Does it work? I'm crushed that you would ask. *Of course* it works. You've done business with M and B many times before, Stanley. You know I would never sell you something that didn't work. Plus there's our unconditional money-back guarantee."

"Not that I don't trust you, but can I try it out?"

"I don't see why not. I'll even give you a nickel."

Tommy put the rag on the table and reached into his pocket. He pulled out a coin, then handed it to Stanley. "Be my guest."

Stanley dropped the coin in the slot and pushed down on the metal handle. A bottle of Coke slid out from behind a black plastic door. Stanley hooked the cap into the opener. The cap popped off and fell into the holder concealed inside the machine's housing. Stanley tilted the bottle to his mouth and took a sip.

"I know what you're thinking," Tommy said. "You're thinking that it's not as good as it used to be, even if it is in a glass bottle. But remember, they stopped using real sugar. Now they use corn syrup or something. It's just not the same."

"It's not bad, though," Stanley said, and took another drink.

"So, do you want to buy it?"

"How much?"

"For you? A mere twenty-five hundred dollars. Anywhere else, a machine like this, in this kind of condition, would set you back at least a thousand dollars more. So this one's a steal, Stanley, a genuine steal."

Stanley didn't like to think of himself as a close man with a dollar, but he wondered just who would be stealing what from whom.

"I'll think about it," he said. "Is Barry around?"

Tommy looked disappointed. "He's in the back. But he won't sell you this machine for a penny less than I will."

"I don't want to talk to him about that. It's about the reenactment."

Tommy's salesman's face turned grim. "That was a real shame about Rance Wofford. He was a customer of ours. But at least you seem to be doing all right. How's your head?"

Stanley leaned over so Tommy could have a look.

"Pretty nasty," Tommy said. "I don't like having stitches."

Stanley didn't like being stitched, either, but he didn't remember having had them. "It looks worse than it is."

Tommy shuddered. "I hope so. Well, if you want to see Barry, go on back. And if you see anything you like on the way, just let me know."

There was something Stanley liked, all right, as Tommy was well aware. It was a forty-year-old Columbia bicycle in wonderful condition. It had been in the store for quite a while now, but so far Tommy and Barry hadn't been persuaded to come down on the price.

Stanley had told himself that he could ride the bicycle for exercise, but he knew he probably never would. He preferred walking, and the bike was really much too nice to ride. He rubbed his hand across the leather seat as he went past it into the back room.

"Still thinking about the bike?" Barry Miller asked when Stanley entered.

"Thinking, yes. Buying, no."

Barry looked away from his computer screen. "Too bad. It's a great bike. Somebody's going to snap it up any day now."

"Maybe. They'll probably take that Coke machine at the same time."

Barry smiled. "I hope so. It would certainly help our balance sheet."

Barry had trimmed his beard and combed his hair back. He looked as much like a movie star as ever.

"I guess Marilyn has already talked to you," Stanley said.

"No, she hasn't."

"No?" Stanley was surprised.

"Don't look so shocked. Marilyn didn't come in person, but Detective Bridger's been here."

Stanley's face changed. "Bridger, huh?"

Barry noticed Stanley's expression. "Bridger's all right."

"Sure, if you like oily guys who've been married three times."

"Just twice, Stanley. And he's not oily."

"Okay. If you say so. What did he ask you?"

"Whether I'd seen anything that might indicate who shot you and Rance. How's the head, by the way?"

Stanley was getting really tired of people asking him about his head. But Barry didn't have any way of knowing that, so Stanley was polite.

"It's great. I'm no more addled than usual. Well, maybe a little."

Barry looked at his computer screen and seemed to consider something there for a second or two. Then he turned back to Stanley.

"You know, you really helped Marilyn out when Belinda was killed. You aren't doing the same thing again, are you?"

Stanley tried not to blush. "Not me. I'm just here out of curiosity."

"If you say so. Anyway, I was no help at all to Bridger. I didn't see a thing. I was wounded."

Stanley looked Barry over carefully. He didn't see anything that looked like a wound.

"Not like you. I was only pretending to be wounded. At the time, it seemed appropriate for my character to fall, so I did. I was on the ground when all the excitement happened."

Stanley was disappointed, but he thought there might be something else Barry could tell him. So he asked if Barry knew of anyone who might have wanted to kill Rance.

Barry wasn't much help. He knew some of the same things that Uncle Martin and Goob had already told Stanley, but he had nothing to add. He was no help with Al Walker, either, even though Walker was an active member of the reenactment group.

"I told you he was a good shot," Barry said. "That's about it."

"There weren't any feuds in the group that you know about?"

"Nothing that I haven't told you."

Oh, well, Stanley thought. He thanked Barry for his time and was about to leave when Barry said, "Uh, Stanley?"

Stanley turned back. "What?"

"I know that you and Marilyn are . . . an item. Isn't that right?"

"I guess you could say that. Why?"

"Well, I don't know whether it's my place to say this, but I think Brad Bridger might be trying to cut you out."

Stanley didn't even try to stop the blush this time. It wouldn't have done any good, anyway.

"What makes you say that?"

"Well, I saw them eating lunch together the other day in the restaurant behind the shop here. It didn't look much like a business lunch, if you know what I mean."

Stanley knew what he meant, all right.

If the heart of a man is depress'd with cares
The mist is dispelled when a woman appears.

—John Gay, *The Beggar's Opera*

I wooed her in the winter time,
Part of the summer, too,
And the only, only thing I did that was wrong
Was to keep her from the foggy foggy dew.

—American folk song

⌒ 15 ⌒

Bushwhacked

It was nearly time for dinner, and Stanley knew that he should go back to the inn, but he was feeling depressed and he thought that talking with Lacy Falk might cheer him up. Besides, if anyone knew the gossip in Higgins, Virginia, it was Lacy Falk. Bushwhackers was right across the street from M & B Antiques, and it was as good as Wooded Acres when it came to hearing loose talk.

When he opened the door, the smell of permanent waving solution and frizzed hair wafted out. Stanley saw Lacy Falk standing behind the cash register that sat on a little wooden counter.

Tammy Vaughn, one of Lacy's employees, was the only other person in the shop. Tammy was thin as a comb, with hair that was teased up about eight inches above her head. She was sweeping hair into a dustpan.

"Hell, honey," Lacy said when she saw Stanley. "What're you doing here? I thought you'd still be laid up in the hospital. How's your head?"

Stanley sighed. "It's fine, just fine."

"Well, I sure thought you were a goner," Tammy said.

"You fell like a load of bricks. Rance, too. But then he *was* a goner." She glanced over at Lacy. "Not that much of a loss, though."

"Not as far as I'm concerned," Lacy agreed. "He was a louse. But you didn't come here to talk about Rance, did you, Stanley? I'll bet you want a haircut. Nothing like a good haircut to perk a man up. It's a little late, though. Tammy and I were just about to go home."

"I don't need a haircut. As a matter of fact, I did come here to talk about Rance."

"Uh-oh," Lacy said. "Sherlock Waters is on the case again."

"It's not like that at all. I just thought that you might have heard something that would throw some light on what happened."

"Honey, if anything happens in this town, I hear about it. Ain't that right, Tammy?"

"Right as raindrops," Tammy said, dumping the hair from the dustpan into a trash basket. "I hear it, too, but I can't stick around to tell you about it. I have a husband that's coming by to pick me up in about ten shakes of a lamb's tail." She looked out through the shop's front window. "In fact, he's out there right now. See you tomorrow, Lacy."

Tammy stood the broom in a corner and left, waving to Stanley as the door closed behind her.

"That girl's always in a hurry. Have a seat, Stanley, and we'll talk."

Stanley sat in one of the metal chairs near the window. He didn't like the uncomfortable vinyl seats, but they didn't seem to bother Lacy. He also didn't like the idea that anyone passing by on the street could look right inside and see him talking to Lacy. He wasn't sure why that bothered him, but it did.

"How'd you like my outfit yesterday?" Lacy asked, making Stanley even more uncomfortable.

"It was a little, ah, revealing."

Lacy laughed. "When you got it, flaunt it, Stanley. And I got a lot of it."

She was indeed a large woman, but she was attractive, Stanley had to admit. If you liked big hair, that is. Lacy claimed that, being from Texas, she was genetically disposed to have big hair.

"You and Rance Wofford didn't get along well, I hear," Stanley said to change the subject.

Lacy's soft mouth got hard. "Damn right we didn't. He was trying to get me out of this building, which I don't blame him for, I guess. It's a great location, right on the main street across from the post office and catty-cornered from City Hall. But I have a lease, and there was nothing he could do about that. He was trying, though. He had him some fancy lawyer from Alexandria, and he was going to take me to court."

"Were you going to lose the space?"

"Who knows? I make good money cutting hair, but I can't afford some fancy lawyer, so I might have. But the truth is, I could've set up somewhere else and done just about as well. I have a reputation, after all."

She had a reputation, all right. She was friendly and outspoken and everyone liked her. Except maybe Rance Wofford. But then maybe he had liked her, too, in a different way.

"So why didn't you just move?" Stanley asked.

"I wasn't going to let Rance Wofford have the satisfaction."

"Someone said that he was a little forward with you. If you know what I mean."

Lacy grinned at him. "Damn, Stanley, you do have a way of putting things. Why don't you come out and ask me if he put his hand on my butt?"

Stanley was turning red again. "Well, I, um, I, ah . . ."

Lacy began laughing. "You're a case, Stanley, you really are. You need to loosen up a little, have some fun. I wish you could see yourself."

Stanley *could* see himself. That was the trouble. The wall opposite the chairs was lined with mirrors where the shop's customers could check out their new hairstyles, and where now Stanley could see his red face staring back at him.

"Don't be embarrassed," Lacy said. "Rance Wofford did put his hand on me, and he made an indecent proposal, too. You want to know what it was?"

"Ah, no, I don't think so. If you don't mind."

"I don't mind. You can imagine what it was, more fun that way. If you have the right kind of mind, that is. Anyway, Rance was just a jerk, is what he was. But I didn't kill him, Stanley. Much as he deserved it."

"You were up on the hill yesterday, though. Weren't you?"

"How'd you know that?"

"Well, um . . ."

"Never mind. I know how. You've been talking to the chief of po-lice. She sent Brad Bridger around here earlier today. Now there's a guy who can put his hand on my butt any day, if you know what I mean. I tried to get him to frisk me for weapons, but he wouldn't. Anyhow, I've already told him all I know. You can check with Marilyn if you want to."

"I'm not working with the police. I'm just interested in what happened."

Lacy looked at him suspiciously. "Everybody in town knows what you did about Belinda. I think you're at it again."

"I'm not, though. I've been told not to mess around in this case. So I'm not, except to try to find out what happened."

"Sure. Well, I was up on the hill, all right. But what could I have shot Rance with? I didn't have a gun."

"You might have hidden one somewhere."

"You saw what I was wearing."

Stanley had seen, all right. But he had already gone over that point with Marilyn, and he didn't see any need to discuss it with Lacy.

"I meant you could have hidden a weapon in the woods," he said.

"Right. I'll bet there've been metal detectors going over that place all day. Have they found anything?"

"I wouldn't know."

"Oh, that's right. You're not working with the police on this. I forgot."

"Right. I'm just curious."

Lacy touched Stanley's shoulder with a fingertip. "Well, I'm a gal who can satisfy a man's . . . curiosity. But you'll have to buy me dinner."

Stanley was tempted, and not just because of the information he hoped to get. But he had to be back at the inn. His guests were expecting him.

"If you're worried about your lady cop friend finding out, I won't tell her. Besides, I think she's slipping around on you."

Stanley started to say something, couldn't think of anything, and just stared.

"You look a little like a frog that somebody stepped on real hard. Do your eyes always bug out like that when somebody takes you by surprise?"

Stanley shook his head and said that he didn't know.

"Well, it's kinda cute, in a way. If you like frogs, that is, which I do. Anyway, I didn't mean to surprise you. I figured you knew about Ms. Chief Tunney and Detective Bridger."

"What is there to know?"

"Nothing, I guess. Sometimes I talk too much. It's an occupational hazard."

"You were going to tell me something about Bridger, weren't you?"

"Well, now that you mention it, I did hear something that might interest you."

Stanley thought things over for a minute. It seemed that there were things going on that he needed to know a little more about. He'd thought that he and Marilyn had some sort of understanding, but obviously he'd been wrong.

Worse than that, everyone in town seemed to know that he'd been wrong.

And even worse than either of those two things was that Marilyn hadn't talked to him about whatever was going on between her and Bridger. If anything was.

She'd seemed concerned about Stanley's head wound, but then maybe the concern was nothing more than anyone would feel for a good friend. Stanley wasn't sure. After all, she'd left the hospital, saying that she had to work the case. The more he found out, the more confused he became.

But he was sure about one thing. He wanted to hear whatever

Lacy had to tell him about Rance Wofford, whether she told him anything about Marilyn and Bridger or not.

So he said, "How would you like to eat dinner with me at the inn?"

"I'd like that a whole lot."

⤳ 16 ⤳

Food for Thought

"You're late," Caroline said when Stanley walked into the kitchen.

"And that's the good news," Stanley said. He could smell collard greens and corn bread.

Bill was sitting at the table. He laughed and said, "I can't wait to see how she takes the bad news."

Stanley could have waited a long time, but he knew that he had to face up to his wrongdoing sooner or later. Putting it off wouldn't help.

"I brought someone to dinner. Lacy Falk."

Caroline was standing at the stove, stirring a mixture of collards and turnip greens in a pot. Her back stiffened.

"Well, I never," she said.

"Go easy on him," Bill said. "This is the first time he's ever brought anybody extra without calling first."

Caroline relaxed. "That's true, so I guess it's all right. I cooked plenty of everything. Bill, you go set an extra place."

Bill stood up and winked at Stanley to let him know how lucky he was to have gotten off so lightly.

"Before I go," Bill said, "you'd better tell me what to do with all the flowers that have been coming in this afternoon."

"Flowers?" Stanley hadn't seen any flowers.

"Plenty of 'em. People must like you a lot, Stanley. We've got flowers coming in from all over."

"*Hello, World!* must have played my concussion up big."

"Probably did. It was probably on the news programs, too."

"Send the flowers to the hospital. They can be put in the patients' rooms."

"Caroline said you'd have some kind of idea like that," Bill said. "So that's what I did."

No wonder I didn't see any flowers, Stanley thought. He thanked Bill and Caroline, and Bill went to set the extra place.

"Your guests have been waiting for you," Caroline told Stanley. "They expected you to be here and talk to them a little. Folks come here for that kind of thing, you know."

Stanley knew, and he generally made it a habit to be around for a while before meals were served.

"Lacy's in there with them now," he said. "She can be pretty entertaining."

"It's none of my business, but I think Chief Tunney might not like you bringing somebody like Lacy Falk here to dinner. Not that there's anything wrong with Lacy. I like her. But you know what I mean."

Stanley knew what she meant, all right. But he didn't want to talk about it.

"I asked Lacy to join us because she knows something about Rance Wofford. I wanted to find out what, and the price was a meal."

"Are you working with the police again?"

"Not officially. I'm just trying to find out why someone would want to kill Wofford."

"Nobody liked that man," Caroline said, putting a lid on the pot of greens. "He never fit into the town."

Stanley added that bit of information to his store and went into the parlor to speak to his guests. Mr. and Mrs. Skidmore were talking and laughing at something Lacy had said, and the other couple, the Heberts from Louisiana, were laughing as well.

"Come on in, Stanley," Lacy said. "I was just telling these fine folks a little about growing up in Texas."

"I'm afraid I don't believe that part about the jackalope," Mrs. Hebert said.

"Swear to God," Lacy said. "Just like a jackrabbit, only about a hundred times as big, and horns like an antelope. There aren't many of them left, though. The one my uncle killed when I was six years old was the last one I ever saw. They've just about disappeared now, like the horny toad."

Bill came in to announce that dinner was ready, and Stanley sighed with relief. He really didn't want to hear the story about the horny toad, if there was one.

The dinner of meat loaf, greens, corn bread, and butter beans was topped off with another pie, lemon meringue this time. The guests raved about every dish, and Stanley called Caroline out of the kitchen to take the compliments.

"Horseradish," she said when asked the secret of the meat loaf.

She had already made one joke that day, so Stanley knew she wasn't kidding. Sheila Skidmore dutifully wrote *horseradish* in a little notebook that she took out of her purse.

After dinner, Stanley, Lacy, and the guests went back to the parlor, where Stanley played a taped episode of *Richard Diamond, Private Detective* for their entertainment.

"I saw that show on TV when I was a kid," Lacy said, though Stanley thought she might have been more than a kid at the time. "I didn't know Richard Diamond sang, though."

"He didn't, not on TV," Stanley said. "Just on radio. Dick Powell was a better singer than David Janssen."

They talked for a while about the TV show, and it was Sheila who recalled that Mary Tyler Moore had played Diamond's secretary, Sam.

"And they only showed her legs," Mr. Hebert said. "Not that I noticed."

"I bet you didn't," his wife said, laughing.

Everyone had a good time, and eventually the Heberts and the Skidmores went upstairs to get ready for bed.

"Now, then," Stanley said to Lacy when the two couples were gone. "I think it's time for us to talk about Rance Wofford."

"If you're sure talking's what you want to do."

Lacy was sitting beside him on the sofa, and she moved closer, nudging him with her shoulder.

"So, are you sure?"

"Uh, sure about what?" Stanley asked, knowing that he was turning red from the top down.

Lacy snuggled closer. Her shoulder felt warm through the thin cloth of her blouse. "Sure you want to talk about Rance Wofford?"

Stanley thought about standing up, but he didn't want to offend her. And after a second or two, he wasn't at all sure he wanted to talk about Rance Wofford. In fact, he was feeling a strong urge to put his arm around her.

But after another moment's thought he realized that he didn't actually know that what people were saying about Marilyn and Bridger was true. It was only gossip, after all, and maybe there was nothing to it. He certainly wasn't going to ask Lacy about it. She might get the wrong idea.

So he said that he really did want to talk about Wofford.

"Oh, all right," Lacy said, sitting up straighter. "But you don't have to be so loyal to the chief of po-lice. I don't think she's as tied down as you believe."

"Maybe not, but I don't want to forget what we came here to do."

"Maybe you came here to talk," Lacy said, patting her hair gently, "but I didn't."

"Rance Wofford."

"Oh, all right. But sooner or later you're going to realize there's more than one fish in the sea, Stanley."

"I probably will. But now that's not what I want to talk about. Are you going to tell me about Wofford or not?"

Lacy moved away from him. "Sure I am. What was it that you wanted to know?"

"I want to know who might have a motive to kill him. Especially if one of the men up on that hill with you might have had a motive."

"I don't know about that. Except for Burl Cabot. His wife's running around on him with Wofford, or I guess I should say she *was* running around on him. Half the people in town knew about it, so I guess Burl's found out by now. He's not as easy to fool as some people I could name."

She gave Stanley a significant look, which he chose to ignore.

"What about Al Walker?" he said.

"Al? He wouldn't kill anybody. Don't think he could, even if he wanted to."

Stanley was close to marking Al off his list. If Lacy didn't know any dirt on him, there wasn't any.

"Neddy Drake?" he said.

"Neddy's not as crazy as you think. He's always talking about that flying saucer, but he doesn't really believe it. He just likes to get attention. He's pretty smart, and he was afraid that if Wofford put in a franchise chicken place across the street from him, he'd lose all his business. He might have shot him for that."

No help there. Stanley had already heard that story. And she wasn't much help with Duffy Weeks, either. All she knew was what Stanley had already heard.

Now it was time for Rance Wofford. It wasn't impossible that someone had loaded one of the rifles without the owner's knowledge, or that someone who hadn't been caught on the tape had been hiding in the trees.

"What other enemies did Wofford have?" Stanley asked.

"Well, there was his uncle, for one."

"His uncle?"

"Think about it, Stanley. A man comes here from nowhere. He's got all kinds of money. He starts buying up property. Doesn't that make you suspicious?"

Stanley said that it didn't. He'd come there with money and bought property, and he certainly wasn't a suspicious character.

"But people know you," Lacy said. "Wofford was a complete stranger."

"He didn't come from nowhere. He made his money in real estate in D.C."

"Are you sure about that?"

"Well, I haven't actually checked up on it to be sure."

"Of course not. Nobody ever did. What if it's just a cover story?"

"For what?"

"You're still not thinking, Stanley. A man that nobody knows or knows anything about. He says he comes from D.C. What does that tell us?"

Stanley had to confess that it didn't tell him a darned thing. "And I still don't know what you mean about his 'uncle.' "

Lacy was exasperated. "Sam. His Uncle Sam."

"He has an uncle named Sam?"

"Sometimes I worry about you, Stanley. I really do. What I'm trying to say is that he worked for Uncle Sam."

Stanley caught on. "But so do a lot of people. Half the people in Alexandria, for instance."

"Maybe so. But not for the CIA."

17

Running Wild

Stanley had plenty to think about as he returned from taking Lacy home. Not the least of which was the way Lacy had grabbed him and kissed him as they stood outside her small brick house.

She'd told him how much she enjoyed the dinner, told him that he was a real gentleman for walking her to the door, then put her arms around him and planted a big, wet kiss on his mouth.

Stanley had been surprised, but he had to admit that the kiss wasn't unpleasant at all. Quite the contrary, in fact.

So he'd slipped his arms around Lacy and kissed her back.

"Now that's more like it," she said. "Want to come in and watch some . . . TV?"

Stanley had resisted. He felt virtuous and silly at the same time. And he wondered more than ever just exactly what his relationship with Marilyn actually was. He told himself that he would never have kissed Lacy if he hadn't heard the rumors about Marilyn and Brad Bridger, but he knew he might have been kidding himself. On the other hand, he'd never thought of himself as especially attractive to women, and now he had two of them to deal with. Or was it only one? It was time for Marilyn and him to have a talk.

The other thing that Stanley had to think about was Rance Wofford's possible connection with the CIA or some other shadowy government agency. If it was true that Wofford had been a government spook, then there were hundreds of reasons why he might have been killed. And none of the reasons had anything at all to do with Higgins, Virginia, or the people who lived there. For all Stanley knew, Wofford could have been killed by the vengeful heirs of some Communist dictator that Wofford had helped overthrow.

Now that the subject had come up, Wofford had looked a little like what Stanley thought a Company man would. He wore suits all the time, had a furtive gaze, and was always glancing over his shoulder.

But looks didn't mean anything. Wofford's dress might have indicated that he was a retired actuary or a former insurance salesman. Stanley had always thought he himself looked more like a neighborhood grocer than a TV weatherman.

He drove up to the inn and parked his car. It was a dark night with no moon, and the sky was speckled with stars. The grounds of the inn were lighted with mercury-vapor lamps that glowed an eerie blue.

Stanley got out of his car and started toward the inn. The blue light washed over him, and his long shadow trailed along behind. He hadn't gotten more than two steps from the car when he heard something that he thought at first was one of the cats crying, but which he realized was actually the high-pitched whine of a car engine.

Something about the sound wasn't right, and Stanley turned toward the main road to see if someone was in trouble.

Someone was, all right, but it wasn't someone on the road.

It was Stanley.

What he saw was a black car about a hundred yards away. It was headed straight for Stanley, not bothering with such niceties as following the normal route to the inn. Its headlights were not on, and it was skimming along over the grass at high speed, bouncing when it hit an uneven spot. After each bounce it landed hard and bounded forward, as if its shock absorbers had long since ceased to function.

Its intent was clear.

It was going to flatten Stanley out on the ground like road kill, or like Wile E. Coyote in some old Warner Brothers cartoon.

Stanley had never thought of himself as a world-class athlete. In fact, he'd never thought of himself as an athlete of any kind, much less one who could outrun a speeding automobile.

On the other hand, he didn't have much choice except to try. At least he had a head start.

He ran in the direction of the inn, thinking that if he could get up on the front porch, he would be safe.

Then he realized that wasn't the case. There were only three steps up to the porch, and the car could easily climb the steps and squash him against the wall like a bug.

Stanley zigged around the corner of the inn and zagged around the compost pile. He was panting now, and sweat was streaming off his head. He suddenly realized why joggers wore headbands.

He didn't have to look over his shoulder to know that the car was only yards behind him. He could hear the weird sound of the highly revved engine. He could also hear the turf thudding against the car's undercarriage as its tires tore great divots out of the inn's lawn.

Stanley's breath was ragged and burning in his throat as he stretched his legs to their limits. A goldfish pond was behind the inn, and he wasn't far from it now. If he could reach it, he was going to try the longest jump of his life.

He saw the sudden sheen of the water and then the toe of his right foot touched the edge of the pond. Taking a deep breath, he threw his whole body up and forward with all the energy he could muster.

If he'd been Superman, or even Batman, it would have been an easy leap to the other side of the pond. He would have glided across like a gull.

But he wasn't Superman or Batman. He wasn't even a gull, and he soared through the air with all the grace and agility of an elephant shot from a catapult.

Luckily the pond wasn't wide, no more than five feet, and Stanley was able to clear the water. When he landed, however, his knees buckled and he pitched forward in an overbalanced run, knowing that he was going to fall, and fall hard.

He put his hands down to catch himself, but his elbows were no stronger than his knees. He found himself rolling over and over in the wet grass.

Behind him, the car nosed hard into the pond, sending up a geyser of water, some of which doused Stanley, who heard the water hiss as it touched hot metal.

The driver threw the car's transmission into reverse. The gears ground, the wheels spun, the engine whined. Then the wheels caught, throwing dirt and grass in all directions.

As Stanley got shakily to his feet, the car backed out of the water. The driver shifted into first gear and swerved around the pond.

Stanley was already running. This time he was headed for the pines and the little stream that flowed in back of the inn.

He didn't think he was going to make it. His lungs were on fire, and he was pretty sure that they were going to pop out of his chest like some alien slime creature.

But that would be preferable to being run over by some drunken idiot who seemed to think the road ran right through Stanley's property.

Stanley pumped his arms and forced his legs to keep moving, though the right one was beginning to cramp up.

When he passed the first tree, Stanley relaxed slightly. No one would be crazy enough to try driving through the woods at night with no lights.

No one, that is, except the person who was chasing Stanley.

The car didn't even slow down, and Stanley heard a sound like a rifle shot as one of the smaller trees splintered under the car's assault.

All right, Stanley told himself, so he's crazy or drunk or he really, really wants to kill me. The smaller trees won't stop him. What I need are bigger trees.

He didn't find a bigger tree, however.

Instead, he tripped over his foot and fell right in the path of the onrushing car.

Stanley lay there panting and said a brief prayer, something that would have sounded like "Dear Lord, please smite the driver of that car with one of your better lightning bolts" if Stanley had been coherent, which he wasn't.

The prayer didn't take long. When it was done, Stanley closed his eyes and waited for the end.

⋐ 18 ⋑

Flip, Flop, and Fly

Stanley fully expected to feel the tires of the car rolling over him and leaving tread marks all the way across his squashed and flattened body.

It didn't happen.

For long seconds, nothing happened at all.

Stanley opened one eye and risked a look in the direction of the car.

It had come to a complete stop. It squatted there, looking like an enormous prehistoric frog. The engine was chugging, and the car vibrated slightly. Stanley wondered if giant frogs vibrated. He imagined the car's grille opening wide and an incredibly elongated tongue flicking out to snap him up like a tasty insect.

That didn't happen, either.

What happened was that the door on the driver's side opened and someone stepped out. No light came on in the car when the door opened, and Stanley could tell nothing about whoever stood there beside the car.

"Get up," Stanley told himself. "You can do it."

Much to his surprise, he could. He wasn't the picture of poise, but he somehow got to his feet.

"All right," he said between gasps. "Come and get me."

The hulking figure beside the car didn't need a second invitation. It moved much more quickly than Stanley thought a human being could, taking four quick strides forward. Then it hit Stanley in the side of the head with a fist approximately the size and hardness of a hubcap.

The blow staggered Stanley and sent him reeling sideways. He slammed into a large tree trunk, a trunk that would have been large enough to stop a tank, much less a car.

Where were you when I needed you? Stanley thought when he bounced off it, wondering what to do next. After all, he wasn't exactly renowned for his ability as a bare-knuckled brawler. In fact, the last fight he'd been in was when he was six years old and someone had tackled him on the playground of Higgins Elementary School. That had been quite a few years and one minor concussion ago.

But he had to do something, so he did what he did best.

He slid down the tree trunk and fell forward, pressing his full length into the damp grass. If he was lucky, his attacker might trip over him in the dark.

He wasn't lucky. The next thing he felt was someone's large shoe kicking him in the ribs.

Stanley groaned and tried to twist away.

He didn't get far enough. Someone kicked him again.

"Forget about Rance Wofford," a husky voice said.

It wasn't a voice Stanley recognized, but the speaker was obviously using an unnatural tone to disguise his normal way of talking.

Stanley turned his head, hoping to see who was kicking him, but all he saw was another foot coming at him—at his head this time.

Stanley didn't really have time to think what would happen if that foot hit him. He simply reacted, grabbing for the foot with both hands.

By great good luck he managed to stop it before it connected. He got his hands around it and twisted.

The foot's owner did an acrobatic somersault over Stanley and landed on the other side of him with a satisfactory thud.

Stanley was at least as surprised as the person he'd just tossed through the air. He staggered to his feet, trying to ignore the pounding in his head. He wasn't interested in finding out the condition of his attacker. If he had a broken neck, that was fine with Stanley, who wanted nothing more than to get to the inn and to a telephone.

He didn't get that far, however. A large hand grabbed the back of his shirt and jerked him off his feet.

Stanley went limp, falling and dragging his adversary to the ground with him. As soon as they hit the ground, Stanley turned and aimed a blow at what he hoped was a tender portion of his assailant's anatomy.

It didn't work out exactly as planned. Stanley hit something hard, the top of a head, and did more damage to his hand than to anything else.

It did seem to stun the attacker, however, giving Stanley enough time to stand up again. Wringing his hand, which was now pulsating in time with his head, Stanley surged forward.

Unfortunately, he'd gotten turned around during the scuffle, and he was no longer headed in the direction of the inn, which he didn't realize until he blundered headlong into the stream.

It wasn't deep, the water coming only to the tops of Stanley's ankles, but it was deep enough to get him soaking wet if he rolled around in it, which is what he did, mainly because he stepped on a small, round pebble, turned his ankle, and fell with a splash.

The water was cold enough to give Stanley a sudden chill, and his instantly sodden clothes seemed to weigh about a hundred pounds.

He got up and flailed around with both arms in the hope that he might accidentally get in a blow before his antagonist hit him again. His fists met nothing but air, however, so he stopped lashing out and stood still. Water dripped off his clothing and off his face as he waited in the darkness for someone to knock him senseless.

Nothing happened for what seemed a long time, though it was probably less than a minute. Stanley looked around and saw no sign of whoever had struck him. There were dark, slinking shadows behind the trees, but nothing else moved.

Except for the rasping of Stanley's breathing, it was as quiet as if nothing had ever happened.

Stanley knew that something had happened, however. His throbbing head and hand were proof enough of that.

Then he heard the sound of the car's engine revving again. The tires threw more dirt as the car backed and filled and then roared off in the direction of the inn.

Stanley stood still for a moment longer. Then he sloshed out of the water and stood on the bank of the stream. His breath was still coming in ragged gasps, and he told himself that he was going to have to get more exercise, maybe walk a little farther each day, build up his lung capacity.

If he lived long enough. Right now, he wasn't sure that he could even walk back to the inn.

Somehow, he made it. It took a while, and he had to stop once to rest, but he finally got there.

He thought at first that he might undress outside to keep the floors clean, but then he thought to hell with that and went on inside, dripping on the floor and tracking mud and grass behind him.

When he got to his bedroom, Sheba was sleeping peacefully in her basket. Cosmo was there, too, but Binky was absent, no doubt roaming around outside.

"Not that he was any help," Stanley told the others. "A fine bunch of watch cats you are."

Sheba and Cosmo didn't move. They just lay there like stuffed cats on a toy store shelf.

Stanley went into the bathroom to take some of the pain pills he'd gotten at the hospital and a shower.

He'd just washed the pills down with water when the telephone rang.

❧ 19 ❧

A Stupid Question

Stanley didn't want to answer it, but it was his private phone, and he thought the call might be important. Besides, he didn't want the ringing to disturb any of his guests in the inn. If they'd slept through the car chase, they deserved to sleep a little longer.

So he picked up the phone. To his surprise the caller was Troy Dresser.

"I didn't wake you up, did I, Stanley?"

Stanley looked down at the water dripping from his clothing and pooling on the floor.

"Not exactly."

"Good. There's something I want to talk to you about."

"Couldn't it wait, Troy? I'm a little busy right now."

Dresser lowered his voice conspiratorially. "A woman?"

"No, of course not. I just need to take a shower."

"This is a lot more important than a shower. It's about Grant Tyler."

"I don't really care about Grant Tyler."

"Not even if he's the one who tried to kill you?"

"Can I call you back?" Stanley asked, suddenly very interested but still very uncomfortable.

"Sure thing," Dresser said, and gave him the number.

*   *   *

Stanley felt much better after a hot shower and after the pills had taken effect. He didn't think he had received any further damage to his head, but he couldn't be sure. He knew that he wasn't thinking entirely clearly, but then a man who'd recently been chased through the woods by a maniacal driver couldn't be expected to be entirely lucid.

He called Dresser back and asked him to explain what he'd meant about Grant Tyler.

"Well, there's a rumor going around up here that you probably haven't heard yet," Dresser said.

Stanley agreed that he wasn't up to speed on industry gossip. He'd never been very interested in it—not even when he was appearing regularly on *Hello, World!*—and he didn't keep in touch anymore.

"You know about the show's ratings, though, don't you?"

Everyone knew about the ratings. They were published everywhere.

"So you know that *Hello, World!* hasn't exactly been setting the world on fire lately."

"I know," Stanley said, wishing that Troy would get to the point. "That's one reason why they did the remote down here, in hopes that it would bring in some more viewers. What does that have to do with Grant Tyler?"

"The word's going around that the network brass aren't happy with Grant. Whether it's fair or not, he's getting the blame for the lower ratings."

"That happens. It's like the quarterback on a football team. If the team loses, the quarterback gets the blame. Or the coaches."

"In our business, the coaches are never wrong," Dresser said. "It's always the players. So the coaches might have to bring in someone off the bench. And guess who the big boys want?"

Stanley had a horrible feeling that he knew the answer to that one. "Me?"

"You. You'd do the weather *and* be the host. And Grant would be shown the door."

"I guess it's a good thing he wasn't up on that hill with a gun."

"How do you know he wasn't?"

It turned out that when the program had gone to the live reenactment, Grant Tyler had disappeared. No one knew where he'd gone, and he hadn't said.

"And no one's going to ask him, either," Dresser said. "If he shot you, it won't be anyone here who finds out."

Stanley sighed. "He didn't shoot me, Troy. Tyler might hate me for some reason, but he wouldn't kill me. And if he did, how would that strengthen his position?"

"Think about it. *Hello, World!* would have all kinds of exclusive footage of you from when you were on the show. We'd play it up really big." Troy paused. "Okay, maybe it wouldn't be as big as the death of Elvis, but it would be big. As it was, you didn't die, but you still got a lot of airtime. Did you see the show today?"

"No, I was in the hospital." Where I should probably be right now, Stanley thought.

"Well, it was great. I'll bet we jumped three or four rating points. Maybe more. And it's like the quarterback situation we just talked about, but in reverse. If the team wins, the quarterback gets to claim credit whether he had anything to do with it or not."

"But I'm not coming back to the show. It's a crazy idea."

"Did anybody ever say that Tyler was completely sane?"

"No," Stanley said. "But there's another problem. I wasn't the target. A man named Rance Wofford was."

"How do you know?"

Stanley gave it some thought. While he was thinking, Dresser said, "Tyler's probably a terrible shot. He could have been aiming at you and hit the other guy."

"Where was he, then? Why didn't he show up in the videotapes?"

"He was hiding."

Stanley didn't believe it, but he didn't disbelieve it, either. "Have you told anyone else about your theory?"

"Are you kidding? I don't want Tyler coming after *me* with a gun."

"I don't think you have to worry. He wouldn't do that."

"Don't be too sure. He got you, didn't he?" Dresser sounded entirely convinced that Tyler was the one who'd shot Stanley.

Stanley, on the other hand, wasn't at all sure. "Grant Tyler didn't shoot me. Don't worry about it, Troy. He wouldn't do it, not even for ratings."

"Everyone knows he hates you."

"He insults me. That's not the same thing. He doesn't try to kill me."

"At least think about it. And watch your back. You might trust Grant, but I don't, not for a minute. He missed once, but he might try again."

"Someone already has."

Here shall he see
No enemy
But winter and rough weather.

—Shakespeare, *As You Like It*, 2.5.1

O wild West Wind,
thou breath of Autumn's being . . .

—Shelley, "Ode to the West Wind"

☞ 20 ☜

The Joy of Joyriders

"You really need to take better care of yourself, Mr. Waters," the doctor said after he carefully checked Stanley's stitches the next morning. "And you should have come here immediately after you fell. How did you manage to fall in a stream, anyhow?"

"I was looking for a cat," Stanley lied. He didn't want word to get around town about what had happened.

"If I were you, I'd just let the cat fend for himself."

"Herself," Stanley said, just to be saying something.

"Whatever. A cat's a cat."

Stanley gave the doctor a doubtful look. He wasn't sure he trusted anyone who didn't like cats.

The doctor caught the look and changed the subject. "You're lucky that you're alive, to tell the truth, Mr. Waters. That's a nice little bruise on the side of your head. What did you say you hit it on?"

Stanley hadn't said. "A rock. When I fell."

The doctor appeared skeptical, but Stanley gave him a bland smile. He wasn't going to change his story. Things were bad enough without everyone in town knowing that someone had tried to kill him the previous evening.

Then again, everyone probably knew already, since the investigation had been performed by none other than Officer Kunkel himself.

After talking to Troy Dresser, Stanley had decided to report what had taken place. He hadn't intended to, but after giving it a little thought, he'd decided he'd better.

His attacker, after all, hadn't been just some random drunk out looking to have a little fun by running over some innocent innkeeper.

There had been a minute or two when Stanley had thought that was the case, but the muttered warning about forgetting about Rance Wofford had erased any possible doubt about the driver's intentions.

So after asking Troy to give Grant Tyler a call to check whether he was in New York, Stanley had called the police.

Geraldine Calloway, the night dispatcher, answered the call. She was hard as nails, and Stanley would have preferred that she do the investigation herself, but she wasn't a sworn officer and didn't do that sort of thing. She informed him that Kunkel was the officer on duty.

"Great," Stanley said with a notable lack of enthusiasm.

Geraldine laughed. "Don't let him arrest *you* for anything."

She had been taking calls when Kunkel had brought Stanley in previously, and she liked to kid Stanley about it.

"I'll try to stay on his good side," Stanley told her, and hung up.

Kunkel had arrived with his siren howling and his light bar flashing. He woke up every guest in the inn. He even woke up all three cats, including Binky, who had come in from his roaming.

The cats weren't bothered for long, however. They just licked themselves a few times, turned around in their baskets, and went back to sleep.

The guests were another matter. About half of them came downstairs, bleary-eyed and wrapped in robes, to see if there was a fire, or if maybe one of the FBI's Ten Most Wanted had checked in for the night.

Stanley assured them all was well and sent them back to bed. Then he dealt with Kunkel, who was as usual decked out in full uniform and bedecked with such items as pepper spray, handcuffs, nightstick, flashlight, radio, and an automatic pistol.

"This had better be the real thing, Waters," Kunkel said, his dislike of Stanley evident in his belligerent tone.

Stanley told him what had happened, then took him outside and showed him the huge chunks of grass and sod that had been gouged out by the attacking car as it pursued him.

After shining his flashlight around for a few seconds, Kunkel took a small spiral notebook from a pocket in his tightly tailored uniform shirt. He held the light under his arm and pointed it at the notebook. His lips moved and he said, "Joyriders," as he painstakingly wrote the word.

"I beg your pardon?" Stanley said.

"Joyriders. You know what they are, right? We've been getting a lot of 'em lately. Kids. It's always kids. You know how it is. They get in dad's car and drive across somebody's lawn and tear it up. It causes the citizens a lot of trouble and gives me a headache. The kids love it. It gives 'em a few laughs, and then they go on somewhere else and tear up another yard."

"It wasn't joyriders," Stanley said, keeping his voice level.

Kunkel straightened and sucked in his belly. He tapped the pencil on the notebook page.

"Who's the professional lawman here? Me or you?"

"You are. And I'm the citizen who nearly got run over and then got his head bashed in."

"The kids were just having fun with you. They wouldn't really have hurt you."

Stanley felt his neck getting hot. That was a bad sign. It meant he was getting angry. When that happened, he didn't redden the way he did when he was embarrassed. Instead, he started heating up somewhere in the area of his esophagus, and the heat rose slowly up his neck, then his face, and finally all the way to the very top of his head. He didn't get angry often, and he didn't like the feeling at all.

"It wasn't kids. Someone got out of the car and hit me. It was a grown-up."

"Sure, sure," Kunkel said in a humoring tone. "I know what you think. Naturally you're a little excited now, but you'll feel different in the morning. Things look better in the light of day. What you need is a good night's sleep. I'll bet we have two or three more complaints tonight about these same kids. I'll catch 'em sooner or later."

Right, Stanley thought. Somewhere around the end of the next ice age.

He said, "Will there be a report of this?"

Kunkel looked insulted and held up his little notebook in front of Stanley's face. "Sure there'll be a report. I took a special class on writing reports. I got the best grade of anybody in it."

Stanley wondered if the other students in the class had been police dogs. He couldn't imagine any other circumstances under which Kunkel could have been the best student.

"Be sure to put in your report that I felt my life was in danger and that I don't agree with you about the joyriders."

"I'm the one writing the report. Did you get a good look at the vehicle?"

Stanley said that he'd gotten a good look but that he couldn't describe the car. He'd never seen one quite like it.

"It was dark. And the car was black. It didn't look like anything I'd ever seen, but maybe if I saw it again, I'd recognize it."

"Can't describe vehicle," Kunkel muttered, writing in his notebook. "I guess you didn't get the license number, either, did you?"

"No. The car's lights weren't on. And I'm not even sure there was a license plate."

"Didn't get license plate number." Kunkel's pencil scratched laboriously across the notebook page as he tried to hold it in the beam of the flashlight.

As he wrote, Kunkel shook his head slowly from side to side. Stanley tried not to notice.

When he'd finished writing down the latest example of Stanley's incompetence, Kunkel said, "What about the kid who supposedly hit you? Did you get a look at him?"

"No one 'supposedly' hit me. I was hit in the head, and I was hit hard."

"Right. Right. I believe you."

Kunkel's tone indicated that he didn't believe a word. He

was talking to Stanley the way he might talk to someone who was mentally incompetent.

"So, if he hit you, you must've seen him. Want to give me a description?"

Stanley was mortified that he couldn't.

"Can't describe alleged assailant," Kunkel said, writing as he muttered.

"Whoever it was, was big."

"Right. That's a big help."

Kunkel closed his notebook, and that was that.

"Well, your head seems all right," the doctor said as if he were a little disappointed that something wasn't seriously wrong. "I wish you'd come in last night, though. You need to be more careful. You're not indestructible, you know."

"I know." As Stanley stood, every muscle in his body seemed to be on fire. "Boy, do I know."

After leaving the doctor's office, Stanley decided to go by the combination city jail and police station to talk to Marilyn. He wanted to see if she'd read Officer Kunkel's report, and if he got the chance, he wanted to discuss some more personal things.

Johnetta Lively was at the dispatcher's desk this morning. Stanley said hello and asked if Chief Tunney was in.

"Yes, sir. I'll buzz her."

Johnetta was a small woman, plain as a pudding, who wore her wiry black hair pulled back into a tight bun. She picked up the phone, pushed a button, and said, "Mr. Waters is here to see you, Chief."

She listened for a second, hung up, and told Stanley he could go right in.

Stanley had visited Marilyn before, and he didn't need any help in finding the office. It was cluttered with papers that were tacked on the wall, lying on the floor, and scattered all over the desk. The ones on the wall were wanted posters, some of them dating back ten years or more. Keeping a neat office wasn't one of Marilyn's strong points.

"It's nice to see you, Stanley," she said when he walked in, sounding as if she meant it. "How's your head today?"

"It's fine. I just had it checked. The doctor says I'll probably live to be a hundred."

Marilyn smiled. "I hope so. Have a seat and tell me what happened at the inn last night."

Marilyn was sitting in one of the two chairs in the office. The other, as usual, had a stack of papers in it. Stanley moved the papers to the floor and sat down.

"Did you read Officer Kunkel's report?"

"First thing this morning. He writes a good report."

"That's what he said. He took a class."

Marilyn nodded. "Top student. Made an A. Did the joyriders do much damage to your grounds?"

"I don't care what Kunkel made in his report-writing class. It wasn't joyriders that tore things up at the inn."

He told her what had happened.

When he finished, Marilyn said, "That's not exactly what was in the report."

"I didn't think it was. That's why I came by. I wanted to tell you the truth."

"Why would Officer Kunkel say something that wasn't accurate?"

Stanley wanted to say, "Because he's an idiot," but he resisted. He said, "I don't know. He doesn't like me, for one thing. Maybe he thought I didn't know what had really happened because I was being hysterical."

"Were you?"

Stanley was so surprised that he didn't know what to say, a rare state for him. He just sat there, looking stunned.

"I didn't mean to be insulting, but Officer Kunkel is a professional."

"That's what he told me," Stanley said, recovering his voice. "He was a professional when he arrested me for breaking and entering, too, but that didn't make him right."

"I see what you mean. So you really think someone was trying to kill you?"

"I *know* someone was."

But Stanley realized that he wasn't really sure. Maybe no one had wanted to kill him at all. Maybe the chase and the hit on the head had just been a warning.

He said as much to Marilyn.

"Even if that's all it was, it must have been a frightening experience," she said.

Stanley started to say that it certainly had been, but he didn't want to look like some kind of sissy. He wanted to look like someone who ate danger for breakfast.

So he said, "It wasn't so bad."

"It sounds like something that should be more thoroughly investigated, at the very least. I'll go out there with you and look things over. Maybe there are some tire imprints that would give us a clue."

Stanley stood up. He was ready to go. Manhunt was his mission. Besides, when they got to the inn, he and Marilyn would be alone, and he'd have a chance to talk to her about other things.

It didn't work out like that, however. Just as they were leaving the office, the telephone on Marilyn's desk rang. Johnetta was calling to say that someone had just tried to kill Burl Cabot.

╒ 21 ╕

A Muffled Shot

Burl Cabot's auto parts store, imaginatively named Cabot's Auto Parts, was only a couple of blocks from the jail.

Marilyn told Johnetta to call for backup. "I'm going over there."

She ran out the door without saying anything to Stanley or looking back. She didn't say, "Stay here, Stanley." Or "Don't try to follow me, Stanley."

So he followed her, except that she took her car, while Stanley walked. He went past the Palace Theater, turned right, and crossed the street. He passed an antique store owned by twin sisters (Twins Antiques) and the post office. He crossed another street, walked past Bushwhackers and a dress shop, turned left, and went through the parking lot of the Baptist church where he'd been baptized. On the other side of the parking lot and across an alley was the parts store.

Two women who worked in the dress shop were walking across the lot toward the street. Stanley knew both of them. One was Jane Gray, who managed the shop. She was about sixty-five and knew the dress size of practically every woman in Higgins. She believed that she had a dress-shop-manager–client privilege, and she would not have revealed the size of any of her customers even if threatened with horrifying death.

The other woman was Francine Wellborn, who was somewhat younger but equally discreet. About dress sizes, at any rate. She was known to talk about other things if the spirit moved her. Stanley asked her what had happened.

"We heard the siren," Francine said.

"And then we saw the police car," Jane added. "So we came to see what was going on. Marilyn ran us off, though. That's all right. We have to get back to the shop."

"She'll run you off, too," Francine said.

"Maybe not," Jane said, and the two women smiled.

They started back to the dress shop, and Stanley told them good-bye. He hoped Marilyn wouldn't try to make him leave. He wanted to know what was going on.

Marilyn's police car was parked in back of the parts store beside a large trash bin. The back of the store had a wide garage door that rolled up and back. The door was wide open, and the dirty, greasy concrete floor of the shop's large back room was covered with old batteries, car parts that Stanley didn't recognize, mufflers, tailpipes, cardboard boxes, and an engine block.

Burl Cabot was sitting on a stack of boxes. Marilyn was talking to him, taking notes in a little book a lot like the one Officer Kunkel had used.

Cabot was wearing a pair of light blue, nearly new jeans and a maroon shirt with some kind of logo on the pocket. He was a huge man. Everything about him was big. He had a big head, big hands, big, broad shoulders. To Stanley, he looked big enough to pick up the engine block and toss it outside.

As Stanley walked up to the door, he heard Cabot telling Marilyn that he had been bringing some old batteries to the back of the store to be picked up for recycling when someone took a shot at him.

Neither Cabot nor Marilyn appeared to notice Stanley, who stood unobtrusively just inside the doorway and leaned against the wall to listen.

"Do you always leave the door up?" Marilyn asked Cabot.

Cabot nodded. "Every day from the time I get here till I close the place up."

"And you think someone shot at you from a car?"

"That's what it was, all right. There's not much place around here where somebody could hide. Anyway, I saw the car."

Stanley looked over his shoulder at the church parking lot. Thick bushes grew along the wall both at the back of the church and along the side of the music store on the other side of the lot. It would have been easy to hide there.

Stanley noticed something else, not that it meant anything. He could see the back corner of Bushwhackers from where he was standing. He wondered if Lacy or someone in the salon had heard the shot.

He turned his attention back to Marilyn, who was asking Burl to describe the car.

Cabot thought for a second. "It's kind of hard to do. It was black, but that's about all I can remember."

A black car that was hard to describe. It sounded familiar to Stanley, but he didn't say so.

"What about a license number?" Marilyn asked.

"The car was all the way across that parking lot, and it wasn't facing me. Besides, when the bullet went by me, I hit the floor. I wasn't looking for any license number."

Marilyn asked where the bullet had struck.

"It went right over my head." Cabot pointed. "It hit those shelves over there, but I didn't take time to see exactly where. I went right to the phone and called you as soon as I picked myself up off the floor."

Cabot was a brave man, Stanley thought, not nearly as shaken at being shot at as Stanley had been by the "joyriders."

"Let's have a look at those shelves," Marilyn said, folding her notebook and putting it in her purse.

The back wall of the large room was lined with metal shelves that held batteries and boxes of parts. Stanley watched as Cabot rummaged through the boxes and pointed out one that had a hole in the side.

"Muffler," he said. "Ford."

Marilyn asked him to lift the box down, which he did. Marilyn looked inside, and after a moment she lifted out the silver-gray muffler.

"The bullet's inside it," she said, giving the muffler a shake. "I'll have to take it to the station."

"Fine with me," Cabot said. "It won't do me any good like it is."

"Do you have any enemies? Anyone who'd have a reason to take a shot at you?"

"Nope. I can't figure it out. I've never done anything to anyone. I can't think of a single reason why anybody would want to shoot me."

Stanley could. Well, not specifically, but there was another person with a connection to Rance Wofford getting his life threatened. A pattern seemed to be developing.

"Did anyone say anything to you?" Stanley asked.

Cabot turned, noticing Stanley for the first time. "Say anything? Heck, no. They didn't stick around for conversation. They just shot at me."

Marilyn seemed about to ask Stanley what he was doing there, but she didn't get a chance. An unmarked car sailed across the church parking lot and squealed to a stop beside the official car Marilyn had driven. Brad Bridger stepped out.

He was wearing a tailored suit, and he looked great in it. Stanley had always admired the way thin men looked in good clothes. Bridger's hair was thick and shiny, and his teeth were either naturally straight and bright or he'd had a good orthodontist when he'd been a youngster.

"Hey, Stanley," he said. "What are you doing here?"

"I just happened to be in the neighborhood. You know me. Trouble is my middle name."

"Right. And danger is your game. But your middle name could be Joe Friday, and that still wouldn't mean you should be getting involved in police business."

Stanley was tempted to say that Joe Friday was two names, not one, but he resisted. It was just as well that he did. Marilyn walked up to them.

"Brad's right, Stanley," she said, but she wasn't talking about middle names. "You really shouldn't be here."

Stanley could have said that he was a citizen and that citizens had a right to visit auto parts stores if they wanted to. But he didn't want to argue about it.

Bridger did. "So you'd better hit the road, Jack."

He stepped forward and tapped Stanley in the chest with his forefinger to emphasize his point. Stanley really hated that kind of thing.

It occurred to Stanley, in fact, that while he had always characterized himself as a sort of modern Will Rogers who'd never met a man he didn't like, he'd recently found himself disliking Grant Tyler, Officer Kunkel, and Detective Bridger. Maybe moving back to hometown America hadn't been such a good idea after all. Maybe it was making him cynical, turning him into a misanthrope.

He gently pushed Bridger's hand aside. "You'd better watch that kind of thing. Someone might accuse you of police brutality. Or plagiarism."

Bridger dropped his hand and stared. "Plagiarism?"

"Stealing lines from Ray Charles," Stanley said in a flat voice that he hoped sounded at least a little like Joe Friday.

Bridger stepped back and glanced at Marilyn as if he thought that Stanley might be going crazy.

Marilyn smiled, but she said, "Stanley, I'm going to have to do some work here, but I'll drive out to the inn later. It could be that what happened out there has some connection to this shooting."

Stanley would have bet on it. He looked around the scene one more time. Something was bothering him, but he couldn't quite pin it down, so he gave it up.

"Do you want to come for lunch?" he asked

He was pretty sure he knew what the answer would be. He was asking only to get Bridger's goat.

"I can't, Stanley. It might be the middle of the afternoon before I get there."

"I'll look forward to seeing you."

Stanley turned and walked away, but not before he caught Bridger's sneer out of the corner of his eye.

Grease

As Stanley walked back through the church parking lot, he decided to stop in at Bushwhackers. He found himself whistling an old gospel tune whose title he couldn't remember. He could remember the important words, however. They had to do with being tempted and tried.

He wondered if his unconscious was being influenced by the proximity of the Baptist church or by the proximity of Lacy Falk. He didn't think about it for long, deciding that self-analysis wasn't going to be a lot of help in this case.

Bushwhackers was busy. All the chairs except Lacy's were full, and both men and women were waiting for the services of Lacy and her assistants.

Tammy Vaughn was there, of course, washing someone's hair. Betsy Rollins was giving Chris Benton a trim. Benton looked a little like a cross between Indiana Jones and Latka from the TV show *Taxi*. His hat sat on the floor beside the chair. Janet Norris was combing out Fran Jenkins, who had a florist's shop a few blocks away.

The TV was tuned to Jerry Springer, who was talking to a woman who looked as if she might have been Officer Kunkel's sister. She had apparently begun dating her stepfather several weeks before his divorce from her mother. Springer was working the audience into a self-righteous frenzy, and Stanley was reminded once again of why he didn't watch much TV these days.

Lacy was standing at the open cash register, going through the bills as if someone had just paid her. Looking up and seeing Stanley, she said, "Hey, there, Stanley. How the hell are you today? Let's have a look at that head."

Several people in the shop echoed Lacy's concern for his head, and Stanley for the first time in his life seriously considered buying a hat. It was either that or go back to the toupee that his producers had insisted he wear during the early part of his TV career. It had been nearly as bad as the one Grant Tyler currently sported, and Stanley had made a vow that he'd never wear it again. So the hat was really his only option.

The trouble with that was that he didn't look good in a hat. Some people did. Brad Bridger was probably one of them. He'd probably look like the leading man in some 1940s film noir. Dick Powell maybe.

But Stanley would look like a cheap gangster. Sheldon Leonard or an inflated Elisha Cook, Jr.

Forget the hat. He'd just have to put up with everyone's concern.

"The head's fine," he said. "Shiny as polished marble, and twice as hard."

He tapped his head gently, and there were a few polite laughs.

"Can you take a break?" he asked Lacy.

"Sorry, honey." She looked it. "I was just on break. Can you come back around noon? I'd love to treat you to . . . lunch."

Something about the way Lacy said things disturbed Stanley. He was never quite sure that he was getting her exact meaning. At other times, he was afraid that he was.

"Just let me make a phone call," he said.

Stanley suggested that they eat at Mom's Crispy Fried Chicken. The food wouldn't be as good as what Caroline had cooked at the inn, and she hadn't exactly been pleased with Stanley's call to let her know that he wouldn't be there for lunch, but Stanley knew that investigators had to make sacrifices in the pursuit of truth.

Mom's was noisy, crowded, and filled with the comforting smell of hot grease. The jukebox was playing a country song about a man whose wife had run off with his truck, his dog, and his gun. "But she left me a six-pack, thank God," the singer wailed. The walls were covered with grease-spattered *X-Files* posters. Stanley was pretty sure that Neddy Drake, the owner of Mom's, thought the show was a documentary.

Neddy was behind the counter, wearing a paper cap and dishing up paper plates laden with fried livers and gizzards, as well as his famous Mom's Lunch Platter: two pieces of chicken, two large biscuits, coleslaw, french fries, and gravy. Behind Neddy, his helpers lowered and raised wire baskets of chicken parts and fries into and out of the bubbling grease that sizzled and popped.

"You can get your cholesterol count up pretty quick in here," Stanley said.

Lacy nodded. "Just by breathing. But fried chicken needs plenty of grease. That's what gives it the flavor."

"I think I'll have the Lunch Platter," Stanley said, giving in to his baser urges. "What about you?"

"I'll take the same. Might as well live dangerously."

Stanley gave Neddy the order. Neddy wrote it on a green pad, tore off the page, and stuck it on a stainless steel ring that spun above the hot grease.

"I'm glad to see that you're okay," he said when Stanley was paying for the lunches. "I was afraid you'd been killed, too. That'd be a real shame."

"Rance Wofford was a shame, too," Stanley said.

"Matter of opinion, I guess," Neddy said, ringing up Stanley's purchase and giving him his change. "I don't think he's any great loss."

"Why don't you join me and Lacy for lunch?" Stanley said. "I'll buy."

Neddy looked at him in disbelief. "You don't think I'd eat this stuff, do you?"

"Well . . ."

"Don't get me wrong. It's great-tasting and good for you, but being around it all day like I am, I don't want to eat it. I haven't had chicken since sometime in 1981. I usually go out and grab a hamburger over at Ed's."

"I'd like to talk to you even if you won't eat," Stanley said. "It's about Wofford."

"Sure. The rush'll be over in a few minutes. I'll join you then."

Stanley took his lunches back to the table where Lacy was sitting. He set them down and asked Lacy what she'd like to drink.

"Anything diet. But not water. I like a little fizz."

Stanley got two cups off the counter and filled them at the soda machine. He noticed several of the patrons looking at him as they ate their chicken, and he was convinced that all of them were wondering about his head. They were all either too polite or too shy to ask, however, and Stanley was grateful for that. He took the drinks to the table and sat down. Then he and Lacy dug in.

Neddy Drake provided plenty of napkins, which was a good thing. By the time he'd eaten a couple of bites, Stanley had grease all over his chin and fingers. He promised himself that in penance he'd ask Caroline to fix vegetarian meals for the next two weeks.

The jukebox was playing another country song, this one about a man whose wife had run off with his best friend. "And I'm sure gonna miss him," the singer declared, just as Neddy walked over to the table.

He was thin, almost skinny, with dirty blond hair and pale blue eyes. His paper cap and apron were blotched with grease stains.

Stanley wiped his mouth with a napkin and told Neddy to have a seat.

"I'm really sorry about what happened, Stanley," Neddy said when he sat down. "I don't know how something like that could go wrong. We've never had an accident before."

"Stanley doesn't think it was an accident," Lacy said, contemplating a french fry. "Stanley thinks somebody shot Rance on purpose. He's playing Sam Spade again."

She bit the end off the french fry and smiled at Stanley, who had never pictured himself much in the Sam Spade mold. He was a lot less tough than Spade. More like an unlettered Philo Vance, maybe.

"You did a good job the last time, Stanley," Neddy said. "Anyway, I don't care if somebody shot Rance. Good riddance, if you ask me."

"Why do you say that?" Stanley asked.

"He was a no-good Yankee. Oh, he had everybody around here fooled, but he couldn't fool me."

"Not that there's anything wrong with Yankees," Lacy said. "Some of my best friends are Yankees. Why, Stanley lived a long time up North, himself."

"But he's not *from* there," Neddy said. "He's from around here. He belongs. He's not like Wofford, coming into town and trying to take over just because he's a Yankee with a lot of money."

"You got any objection to people having a lot of money?" Lacy asked.

"No," Neddy said. "Just to pushy Yankees."

"Damn, honey," Lacy said. "He was trying to run me out of my business, too, but that's no reason to be glad he's dead. And it's no reason to speak ill of the man after he's gone. That's bad luck or something."

Neddy didn't pay her any mind. "Rance Wofford was mean, and he was vicious. He was going to run me out of business, and he made fun of me to everybody. He came in one night and told all my customers that I was crazy."

Stanley looked around at all the *X-Files* posters and tried to think of something to say.

Neddy saved him the trouble. "I know half the town thinks I'm crazy, but—"

"I'd say it was more like three-fourths of the town," Lacy told him. She took a sip of her diet cola. "If you want to be accurate about it."

"Doesn't matter. Heck, I don't even blame them. Who'd believe that someone could be abducted by a flying saucer, anyway? Until it happened to me, *I* wouldn't have believed it. But that's not the point. The point is that Wofford had no business coming in here and trying to drive off my customers. He was lucky I didn't shoot him right then. It's a good thing I don't keep a gun on the premises, or I'd have been strongly tempted."

"Uh," Stanley said, "does that mean you did shoot him the other day?"

"Of course not. I wouldn't shoot even a pushy Yankee without giving him a fair chance."

Stanley wondered just what Neddy would consider a "fair chance," but he didn't ask. Instead he said, "If you didn't shoot him, do you know who did?"

Neddy looked around, saw that no one was looking in their direction, and said, "Sure."

⌒ 23 ⌒

Grease II

Lacy laughed and wiped her fingers with a paper napkin.

"Damn, honey," she said to Stanley, "I bet he's gonna tell you it was some Martian."

Neddy gave her a resentful look. "You're as bad as Wofford."

"I hope that doesn't mean you're going to kill me, too," Lacy said.

"I didn't kill anyone, and it wasn't 'some Martian' that killed Wofford. It wasn't even someone from outer space. It was Duffy Weeks."

Stanley was excited. "How do you know?"

"I don't really *know*. But I'm sure of it. Duffy'd been talking about it for days."

Stanley wondered why no one else had mentioned this important fact to him if indeed it was a fact.

"You don't believe me, do you?" Neddy said.

"We believe you," Stanley said, with a warning glance in Lacy's direction. "I mean, we believe it wasn't someone from outer space. I'm not sure I believe it was Duffy Weeks, though."

"You can believe what you want to, then. We all talked about Wofford the night before, and—"

"Hold on a minute," Stanley said. "Before what?"

"Before the reenactment. A bunch of us camped out the night before, and we talked about Wofford and how pushy he was and how he was ruining Higgins."

"Where did you camp?"

"Not far from the inn. Didn't you see the campfires?"

Stanley remembered that Caroline had mentioned the fires.

"Yes," he said. "Who was camped with you?"

"Duffy, for one. And Burl and Al."

"Wofford wasn't there?"

Neddy laughed. "Heck, no. He never socialized with us. He was too good for that."

"And so you talked about him?"

Neddy looked a little frustrated. "That's what I just told you. We didn't like what he was doing to the town, the way he was buying up all the buildings." Neddy leaned across the table. "And you know what comes after that, don't you?"

Stanley wasn't sure he knew. He looked at Lacy for a clue, but she just shrugged.

"I don't think I know," Stanley said. "You're going to have to tell me."

"Then he starts modernizing," Neddy said. "You take that hotel he's bought. How long has that building been there?"

Stanley remembered seeing the construction date on the hotel's facade, but he didn't know what it was.

"Since 1885," Neddy said. "That's how long. And what do you want to bet he'd tear it down and build some kind of monstrosity like the City Hall. It's just what a Yankee would do."

To Stanley, and to most of the current residents of Higgins, the City Hall was an example of what happens when someone decided that a community needs an updated image. It was an example of 1950s "modern," and it didn't go well at all with the rest of a town with many nineteenth- and early-twentieth-century buildings. The old City Hall had been demolished and now existed only in photographs and memories.

"You can't be sure that would happen," Stanley said.

"You can't trust a Yankee," Neddy said darkly. "Not even one that likes to dress up like a Confederate. Al Walker's president of the preservation society, and he says that Wofford had been talking to people about making changes in the town. Al was really upset about it."

So now even Al Walker had a motive to kill Wofford, Stanley thought.

"In fact," Neddy went on, "I think he was the one who said Higgins would be better off if Wofford had never come to town. And that's when Duffy said that since Wofford was already here, we'd be better off if he'd just drop dead."

"That's not exactly the same thing as shooting him," Stanley said.

"No, but that's when we started talking about it."

"About what?"

"About shooting him."

"Who brought it up?"

"I don't remember. It was just joking, at first. Duffy had been drinking some, like he's been doing lately. Well, it wasn't just Duffy. We'd all been drinking a little, to tell the truth, and somebody said maybe if Wofford got shot, all our troubles would be over."

"Who said that?"

"Who knows? We were joking, like I said. It didn't mean anything."

"It might have to someone. Wofford's dead, after all."

"Like I said, we were just kidding around. Nobody really meant for him to get killed, but we were all going to shoot at him. Even that TV guy thought it was funny."

Stanley jumped. "What TV guy? You didn't mention any TV guy."

"Well, you didn't ask. You asked who was camping out, and I told you. The TV guy just showed up. He said he saw the fires and thought he'd see what was going on."

Stanley vaguely remembered hearing someone or something on the stairs the night before the shooting. He'd thought it was one of the cats, but he'd been wrong. It had been someone even sneakier than a cat.

"So he heard you talking about shooting someone?"

"Well, he could have. Maybe he wasn't there then. I don't really remember. Anyway, what difference does it make whether he was there or not? We were just joking about shooting at him, that's all."

"It wasn't a joke the next day."

"That night it was. It was all in fun, you know? We weren't going to have loaded weapons, so what would it hurt?"

"Somebody's weapon was loaded."

"Sure. Duffy's. I told you he did it."

"How do you know?"

"He told me."

"He *told* you?"

"That's what I said." Neddy looked concerned. "Do you have a hearing problem, Stanley? Sometimes a concussion can cause that, you know."

Stanley didn't know what concussions could cause, but he didn't have a hearing problem, though it wasn't easy to talk with the chatter in Mom's, and with the jukebox blaring out yet another plaintive ballad about a man whose wife spent all her time in "smokey bars and smokey cars" or "walkin' under smokey stars" with men who weren't her husband or even his best friends.

"I heard you just fine," Stanley said. "When did Duffy tell you this?"

"Last night. I went by the tavern for a beer after I closed down here, and Duffy said he shot Wofford. He said he was glad he did it, too."

Stanley was suddenly eager to talk to Duffy Weeks, but he had a few more questions for Neddy first.

"Have you told anyone else about this?"

"Who would I tell?"

"The police."

"Who, that Brad Bridger? He came by the house and questioned me last night, but I didn't tell him a thing. I wouldn't give him the time of day. I don't think you should, either, Stanley, not that it's any of my business."

Stanley had lost the thread of the conversation. "What's not your business?"

"That Brad Bridger is beating your time with the chief of police. There, I've said it."

"Don't worry, Neddy," Lacy said, smiling. "Stanley's already been told. Haven't you, Stanley?"

Stanley ignored her. He didn't want to discuss his personal life just now. In fact, he didn't ever want to discuss it with Neddy Drake. Maybe with Lacy, but not until after he'd sorted through his feelings.

So he said to Neddy, "Did Duffy happen to tell you why he shot Rance?"

"No. He just said that he did it. I didn't ask him why. I thought that was a little personal."

"Wofford was putting the squeeze on Duffy, too," Lacy said. "Trying to get him to sell out. He was trying to buy up the whole town, if you ask me."

"That's not all," Neddy said.

Stanley had been almost ready to leave, but he changed his mind. "What else is there?"

"I don't know for sure, but Duffy was real upset at the campout. He wouldn't talk about it, but it was more than just his tavern that he was worried about. We could all tell it was something pretty bad."

"But you don't know what it was."

Neddy shook his head, and Stanley got up to leave. The jukebox was playing yet another weeper, this one about a man whose wife had left because she loved "roughnecks, longnecks, and rednecks" more than she loved him.

"What about you, Lacy?" Stanley asked. "Any ideas?"

Lacy shrugged. "Not a one. As far as I know, Duffy's problems are the same as mine."

Stanley turned to Neddy. "Any more surprises for us before we go?"

Stanley knew that his next stop would be Duffy's Tavern, but he wanted to be sure that Neddy didn't have any more revelations for him.

"Now you know all I know," Neddy said. "And a lot more than the cops know, if they were hoping to learn it from me. I don't have any respect for a man that's trying to beat somebody's time. Besides, I'd rather help you than the cops. I really admired what you did when Belinda was killed."

"Thanks," Stanley said, though he didn't think it was a good idea to have people thinking of him as some kind of investigator. He took Lacy's arm, and they left Mom's just as the opening notes of a new tune sounded from the jukebox.

"I sure wish I didn't have to go back to work, Stanley," Lacy said. "It's a real pleasure to watch you sleuthing. But Miss Odell is coming in for a perm, and she won't stand for anybody but me to do it."

"I think I'm about through sleuthing for the day," Stanley lied. "I'd better tell Bridger what Neddy said and let the police handle things from here on in."

Lacy punched him lightly in the arm. "You sure are a case, Stanley. You know you're not going to let that Bridger in on anything, not until you've checked it out yourself. I know you better than you think."

She obviously did. Stanley wondered about that. Was he so easy to figure, or did women like Lacy just have a knack for reading men's minds?

She didn't tell him. She said, "You can give me a call later if you want to. We could get together tonight and have a long . . . talk."

As she walked away, leaving Stanley standing on the walk in front of Mom's Crispy Fried Chicken, he wished he didn't still suspect that she might have had a hand in the murder of Rance Wofford.

⌒ 24 ⌒

A Seat on the Square

Nothing was very far from anything else in Higgins. As a matter of fact, Duffy's Tavern was just down the street from Neddy's place.

But Stanley didn't go immediately to the tavern. Instead he crossed over to the town square. It was a beautiful day, warm and sunny, the kind of day that weathermen liked to forecast and liked to take credit for when the forecast was right. Stanley wasn't really enjoying the weather, however. He had too much on his mind. He hoped to find an empty bench on the square so that he could sit down and think for a while.

He found one almost immediately, not far from the statue of the Confederate veteran that stood in front of Higgins's "modern" City Hall. He sat down and looked over at the statue. The soldier didn't look back, of course. He was looking off somewhere into the distance, posed as if he might be walking back home after a long, hard campaign.

Stanley turned away from the soldier and watched a gray squirrel skitter across the square. It ran toward the street, turned back when it saw a black Ford passing by, and ran up an oak tree.

Stanley felt like hiding in a tree himself. He liked investigations, but he didn't like thinking that his friends or people whom he knew might be murderers.

Lacy, for example. He was pretty sure she hadn't been the person he'd fought with the night before, but she might have an accomplice. And she'd been on break when someone had taken a shot at Burl Cabot, who'd seen some kind of indescribable car. Like the one that had chased Stanley.

Speaking of cars, Stanley thought, there was that black Ford again, the one that had scared the squirrel. Tourists, probably, and probably lost. He looked more closely, but he couldn't tell anything about the car's occupants. The windows were too darkly tinted for him to see inside.

He remembered something that Lacy had said about Wofford's having worked for the CIA. He wondered if the car might be occupied by two men in dark suits. Or was that the FBI? The CIA wasn't supposed to operate within the borders of the continental United States, was it? But maybe that didn't count if one of their former operatives had been murdered.

By the time Stanley reached that point in his speculations, the car had gone on down the street, past the Palace Theater and the jail and out past the high school and Wooded Acres and out of town. If it didn't turn and come back.

Stanley sat quietly for several minutes, not thinking about much of anything as he waited for the car to return. He listened to the squirrel chittering away somewhere in the branches of the tree it had climbed, and he saw any number of cars go by, some of them owned by people he knew. No one noticed him sitting near the statue, however.

After a while Stanley decided that the black Ford wasn't coming back. He'd been imagining things again. The car was black, but it certainly didn't look a thing like the one Stanley had fled from. He'd been right about the tourists, after all. They'd made a couple of turns around the square, and now they were on their way elsewhere to do more sight-seeing.

Stanley turned his thoughts back to Lacy. She was an attractive woman, no doubt about it, though she was very different from Marilyn. And she clearly liked Stanley, maybe more than liked him. He found that both flattering and a little frightening.

Part of the fright was caused by the fact that Stanley still had strong feelings for Marilyn, and he wasn't entirely convinced that her relationship with Brad Bridger was anything more than purely professional. Couldn't she have had a business lunch with him? People did things like that all the time. Cops had to talk things over now and then, didn't they?

Anyway, Stanley thought that Marilyn still liked him. He was almost convinced that her desire to keep him out of the investigation into Wofford's death was caused by her concern for his safety.

After all, what if he had been the target?

That reminded him that he hadn't heard from Troy Dresser about Grant Tyler's whereabouts. Could it have been Tyler in the black Ford? The Ford would certainly have been an effective disguise for Tyler, who preferred to drive flashy cars such as red Chrysler convertibles.

Telling himself that he'd give Troy a call later on, he stood up and stretched. He was about to head for Duffy's when he saw the black Ford again.

All the windows were rolled up, so no gun was protruding from the car. It drove along the street at a steady pace, not speeding but not going particularly slowly, either.

Maybe it was only Stanley's imagination, but the car seemed to slow down when it drew even with him, as if someone inside were being sure to get a good look.

Then the car pulled over to the curb and stopped. Stanley felt as if he'd suddenly grown a little bull's-eye right in the middle of his forehead.

The passenger-side window slid down. Stanley looked for a place to hide, but there was no place to go. He thought about ducking under the bench, but that would have been too undignified. Better to get shot right where he was standing.

His shoulders tensed as he awaited the bullet.

It didn't come. Instead someone called from inside the car, "Sir, could you please tell us the right road for Wooded Acres?"

Stanley slowly relaxed. Then he walked over to the car.

"Did you say Wooded Acres?"

He could see inside the car now, and a blond woman was

sitting in the passenger seat. A man was driving, and two children were in the back.

"Yes," the woman said. "Wooded Acres. My grandmother is there. We're from Richmond, and we've never visited here before. My husband didn't want to bother you, but I made him stop."

"You were going in the right direction," Stanley said. "You probably drove right past it."

"I told you so," a voice from the backseat said. "I told you that's what the sign said."

The blond woman turned to the back and said, "Never mind. We can go right back." She looked at Stanley again. "Say, aren't you Stanley Waters?"

Stanley admitted that he was.

"How's your head?"

Stanley sighed and told the woman that it was fine.

"Well, you take care of yourself. You're our favorite weatherman."

The window rolled up, and the car rolled away. Stanley laughed at himself for thinking it might have had some connection to the CIA. Rance Wofford was probably exactly what he appeared to be, a businessman who'd seen a chance to make money in Higgins. There was no CIA connection. Stanley had a strong feeling that the reason for Wofford's death was right in Higgins, Virginia.

Stanley started to walk toward Duffy's Tavern, but then he glanced toward Jamar's funeral home. He thought it would be a good idea, before he went to Duffy's, to stop by Jamar's and say his last good-bye to the late Rance Wofford.

For they have sown the wind,
and they shall reap the whirlwind.

—Hosea 8:7

And now there came both mist and snow,
And it grew wondrous cold.

—Coleridge, *The Rime of the Ancient Mariner*

⮜ 25 ⮞

Fine and Private Places

Jamar's was located next door to Mom's, an unusual juxta-position but one that pleased Stanley's sense of aesthetics. He walked through the front door onto the hardwood floor that looked as if it had just been polished that morning. Before he had finished signing the visitors' register, John Jamar was stand-ing beside him.

Jamar's sudden, soundless appearance didn't startle Stanley. He'd been expecting it. He didn't know how Jamar did it, but he could appear so noiselessly at your side that it was almost as if he'd materialized out of thin air.

"Good afternoon, Mr. Waters," he said, his voice soft and hushed yet still clearly audible. "Are you here to visit Mr. Wofford?"

Stanley nodded.

"Follow me."

Stanley was grateful that Jamar hadn't asked about his head.

Jamar was small and neat and immaculately dressed. Not so much as a spot of dust was on his dark suit and white shirt, nor was there even the tiniest scuff on his highly polished shoes. Stanley felt slightly guilty, knowing that somewhere on his Dock-ers there were bound to be traces of the grease whose scent still clung faintly to him despite the time he'd spent in the fresh air of the square.

Jamar led Stanley to the Rose Chapel, the same room where Belinda Grimsby had been placed. Stanley hoped there would be no embarrassing incidents of the kind that had occurred when he'd paid a last visit to her.

It didn't seem likely. Only two people were in the room, and Stanley didn't recognize either of them.

"Mr. Wofford's sisters," Jamar said in a whisper that was meant for Stanley's ears only. "They just arrived from Florida. They're his only relatives. They made all the arrangements."

Stanley, remembering what Goob and Uncle Martin had said about following the money, wondered if the sisters were also Wofford's heirs. If so, he wouldn't have to worry about following the money. The sisters couldn't very well have killed Wofford if they were from Florida.

Stanley spent a few minutes at the back of the room, listening to the hymns that were piped in on the sound system. He heard slow versions of "Leaning on the Everlasting Arms" and "In the Garden," then went down and offered his sympathies to the sisters. They thanked him, and he left. He wasn't going to learn anything there, and he didn't need to spend any time with the body. He knew that Wofford was dead.

Jamar didn't appear beside him again, and Stanley found his own way outside.

Duffy's Tavern had a jukebox, but the selections were completely unlike the ones in Mom's. They were unlike the selections in Jamar's, too, for which Stanley counted himself lucky. They leaned mostly toward slow ballads by the likes of June Christy, Julie London, Gogi Grant, Jo Stafford, Doris Day, and Peggy Lee. Stanley liked all those singers, and he liked ballads, but he hoped that to liven the afternoon up someone would play Gogi Grant's version of "The Wayward Wind."

It didn't seem likely. When Stanley walked inside, the dimly lit bar was quiet. The only two customers in the place, a man and woman whom Stanley didn't recognize, sat in a booth in the back and seemed wrapped up entirely in their conversation.

Duffy was behind the counter, reading an old copy of *Entertainment Weekly* with Brad Pitt on the cover. Duffy put the magazine down when Stanley came through the door.

"What can I get for you, Stanley?"

Stanley took a seat on a barstool. "Bud Light," he said, though he usually didn't drink beer.

Duffy pulled out a bottle and popped the top. Then he set the bottle on the counter along with a napkin and a glass. Stanley poured the beer into the glass and took a drink.

"Not bad," he said.

"If you like light beer. Which I don't."

It was obvious, however, that Duffy liked something. If his hand hadn't been shaking just the least little bit, he might have poured Stanley's drink for him.

Stanley looked around the bar. Duffy didn't go in for neon or flashy decor. Just lots of dark wood, leather, and glass, which was fine with Stanley. He didn't like neon, either.

"Things going all right, Duffy?"

Duffy didn't answer. He looked down as if he'd like to pick up his magazine and read about Brad Pitt, or maybe he was just avoiding Stanley's eyes.

"I was just talking to Neddy Drake," Stanley went on. "He says you and some of the guys camped out the other night before the reenactment."

"Yeah," Duffy said, still looking down. "We like to do that sometimes."

"He said that Grant Tyler paid you a visit."

"Yeah. That was great. I mean, how often does someone like me get to talk to a real TV star."

Stanley tried not to look hurt, but Duffy must have noticed a change in his expression.

"Well, I get to talk to you all the time, but you're not on TV anymore."

"Never mind," Stanley said. "Did Tyler join in the talk about Rance Wofford?"

"He didn't know Rance, did he?"

"I don't think so. I was just wondering what he had to say."

"You know what we were talking about?"

Stanley rested his elbows on the bar. "Neddy told me."

"We were joking around, that's all. Maybe we were trying to impress Mr. Tyler. Someone said it might be a good idea to shoot Rance and get him out of our hair once and for all, and Mr. Tyler joked that it might improve his show's ratings if we did."

Stanley thought about that for a second or two. It put things in an entirely new light. Maybe Tyler was involved, but not in any plot to kill Stanley. Now even Tyler had a motive to kill Rance Wofford.

"So you all decided to aim for Rance," Stanley said. "Just in fun, of course."

"Sure, that was it. Just in fun. We'd all point our rifles at him and fire. But it wouldn't hurt him, since the guns weren't loaded."

"So that's what you did."

Duffy nodded. "That's what *I* did. I can't say about any of the others."

"Neddy told me something else. I thought I'd better ask you about it."

"What's that?"

Stanley looked at the two customers, a man and a woman who were still engrossed in each other. They probably weren't even aware that Stanley was in the room.

Stanley looked back at Duffy. "It was about you."

"I was pretty drunk that night, if that's what you mean."

"Neddy mentioned that everyone had had a little to drink."

"I was a little drunk the next morning, too."

"You start early, don't you?"

Duffy sighed. "Yeah, I do."

"This wasn't about your drinking, though. Neddy says you told him something later, something about Rance Wofford."

Duffy's eyes slid away from Stanley. "I might have. I don't remember."

"You'd remember this."

"I don't remember so good these days. Look, Stanley, I like talking to you and all, but I've got customers to take care of."

"They look pretty happy to me."

"Yeah, but that's because you're not a professional. I can tell they need refills. I'll be back in a minute."

Duffy went over to the booth, spoke briefly to his customers, who apparently didn't need refills after all.

Duffy returned to his place behind the bar. But not to the same place. He stopped a couple of stools away from where Stanley was sitting and started stacking glasses on the shelf underneath the bar.

"I guess they didn't want anything," Stanley said.

"Nah. I was wrong. Even a professional makes mistakes now and then."

Stanley left his hardly tasted beer where it was and moved over to sit in front of Duffy, who didn't look up.

"Have you talked to Brad Bridger yet?" Stanley asked.

Duffy dropped a glass on the floor. It didn't break because a thick black rubber mat was down there, but it rolled around for a second. Duffy picked it up and put it back on the shelf.

"Well?" Stanley said.

"He came by. We talked."

"Did you tell him you killed Rance Wofford?"

Duffy looked up with alarm. "No. Of course not."

"You told Neddy that you killed him, though. Right?"

Duffy sighed and his shoulders slumped. "Yeah. I guess maybe I did."

"You guess what? That you told him or that you did shoot Rance?"

Duffy looked sheepish. "Well, it's hard to say about either one of those things. These days, I'm not real sure about anything."

"So you don't know whether you shot Rance, and you don't know whether you told Neddy about it."

"That's right. I guess I did, though, if he said so." He paused, then said, "And Stanley?"

"What?"

"If I did shoot Rance, I'm real sorry about your head."

⌐ 26 ⌐

No Promises

Duffy might have been sorry about Stanley's head, but he didn't want to discuss Wofford's death. "I can't talk about it. Not here, and not now. Excuse me, Stanley, but I have something I need to do."

He walked to the table in back to check on his customers and then disappeared through the door that led to his office. When he came back, his smile was brighter and his step was lighter. It didn't take Philo Vance to figure out what he'd needed to do in the office.

But Stanley didn't comment on that. He said, "I really need to know the whole story, Duffy. I might be able to help you."

"You can't help me, Stanley. I probably shot the guy, and if I did, then I'm glad I did. He deserved it if anyone ever did."

"Sooner or later Brad Bridger's going to hear the same things I've heard. And when he does, he'll come after you."

That idea seemed to bother Duffy, but only for a moment.

"If he comes after me, then he can have me." Duffy held up an unsteady hand and stared as it gave a slight twitch. "I probably belong in jail. If I were there, maybe I could get myself straight."

"Why the drinking, Duffy? I've known you since I moved back here, and you've never had a problem before."

"It's Wofford."

"But Wofford's dead."

"Then maybe that's why I'm drinking."

Stanley shook his head, angry at Duffy for being so stubborn. "You're going to have to tell me the whole story. Either that, or I'm going to tell Marilyn. And I wish you wouldn't make me tell her. I just don't believe you killed anyone."

"What would you know? I've fired that rifle a lot, Stanley, and I know what it's like. Dry firing's different from firing a loaded weapon. I can tell the difference. Anyone who's familiar with a rifle can tell."

"But you loaded the rifle. Why would you put a bullet in it?"

Duffy looked at Stanley. "I don't remember whether I did or not, to tell you the truth. And if I did, I don't know why. I told you: I was drunk."

And that was all he would say. More customers began to come in, and the bar got busy. Duffy moved away from Stanley and didn't come back until Stanley finally beckoned him over.

"I have to find out the whole story," Stanley said. "It's the only way I can help you."

Duffy thought for a moment. "All right. I give up. I'll tell you. But not here. My relief man comes on at eight. Come by my house sometime after that. Maybe I'll feel like talking then."

"I'll be there."

"I'm not making any promises," Duffy said to Stanley's back as Stanley headed for the door.

Stanley walked back to the police station to pick up his car. He thought about going in to see Marilyn, but then he changed his mind. He didn't know what to say to her.

He was getting into his Lexus when she walked out the front door and called to him.

"Stanley! Where have you been? I've been looking all over for you."

Stanley stepped back out of the car. "I've just been fooling around town. I had lunch at Mom's."

Marilyn eyed him suspiciously. "Did you talk to Neddy?"

"A little. I wasn't prying into the case, though."

Stanley knew that he wasn't a practiced liar, but he was getting better at it, and he hoped he could fool Marilyn. He couldn't, however.

"I can tell when you're lying, Stanley. Your face always gets a little red."

"I wasn't doing anything dangerous. Not unless you count eating Neddy's chicken."

Marilyn laughed. "That can be hazardous to your health, for sure. All right, Stanley, I'll forgive you this time. But don't go prying into things. You saw what happened at Burl's today. So promise you'll keep out of this."

"All right," Stanley said, hoping his face wasn't giving him away again. "But weren't we going out to the inn to look things over? Check out those tire tracks?"

"We were. But I'm tied up right now. I can drive out there later. Would that be all right?"

"Sure. I wanted to go visit my uncle, anyway."

"How is Martin?"

"He's fine. He'll probably be around for another fifty years."

"I hope so. Tell him I said hello."

"I will."

"And that friend of his, Goob. Tell him, too."

Stanley said that he would, and then he got in his car and drove away.

Jeopardy! was on again, but Goob and Uncle Martin weren't interested in it at all. They wanted to hear what Stanley had learned. It wasn't much, but he filled them in on what he thought they needed to know, including the attempt on Burl Cabot's life, and told them what had happened at the inn.

"That Kunkel oughta be made the dogcatcher," Goob said. "Maybe he could handle that."

"They call it 'animal control officer' these days," Stanley said. "And it requires plenty of intelligence."

"They could fire him, then," Uncle Martin said. "Joyriders, my foot. Somebody's out to kill you, Stanley. You'd better watch your back."

"If they'd wanted to kill me, they could have. Someone just wanted to scare me. And it worked."

"Now I don't believe that," Goob said. "You don't look scared to me."

Stanley had to admit that he wasn't scared at all. He probably should have been, but he wasn't. He was more angry than anything. He didn't like to be bullied.

"Marilyn is coming out later this afternoon to check things out," Stanley said. "We'll walk over the grounds, maybe even check out the area where Wofford was shot. You never know. We could get lucky and find something."

Uncle Martin and Goob gave one another significant looks.

"What's that supposed to mean?" Stanley asked.

"What's *what* supposed to mean?" Uncle Martin said.

"That look. What are you two up to?"

"Not up to a thing," Goob said. "We were just wondering about you and the chief, that's all."

"Well, you can stop wondering. There's nothing to wonder about."

"About her and Brad Bridger," Uncle Martin said. "That's what we were wondering about. And whether you said anything to her."

Stanley shook his head. "I didn't say a thing. I didn't have a chance. Maybe I'll talk to her later this afternoon, and maybe I won't."

"Better forget about her," Uncle Martin advised. "A woman that'll sneak around behind your back and go out to eat with another man, that's not good."

Stanley thought guiltily about his lunch with Lacy, and about his dinner with her the previous evening. But that wasn't exactly the same thing. Was it?

To change the subject, he said, "What about Burl Cabot's mother. Do you think she knows about the shooting?"

"We'll tell her," Uncle Martin promised. "After you've gone. You might upset her, but we know how to handle her. That's her sitting right over there."

He motioned toward a woman sitting in a wheelchair and holding a paperback book. Stanley couldn't see the title.

"Burl's sure good to visit her," Goob said. "Not like some people I could name."

Stanley wasn't interested in who came for visits. He said, "Do you two know about the preservation society?"

"That thing Al Walker heads up?" Uncle Martin said. "What's that got to do with anything?"

Stanley told him.

"I see what you mean," Uncle Martin said when Stanley had finished. "Those preservation folks can get downright fanatical about old buildings. They want to save their heritage, or so they say. They don't seem to mind much, though, when old folks like me and Goob get stuck off in places like this."

He waved a hand, and Stanley looked around the room. Several people were lively and happy, but others weren't. They sat slumped in wheelchairs where they faced the TV set but saw nothing of Alex Trebek and the *Jeopardy!* players. They didn't have any visitors.

"We old guys aren't like buildings," Goob said. "Nobody wants to look at us. Nobody even wants to be reminded of us."

"Marilyn does," Stanley told them. "She wanted me to say hello for her."

"She's okay," Goob said. "If she didn't slip around with other fellas, that is."

"We're getting off the subject," Stanley said.

"Yeah," Uncle Martin agreed. "Well, those preservation folks aren't above a little violence. I remember something that happened a couple of years before you moved back, Stanley. It was when Corey Gainer bought the old Palace Theater."

Stanley liked the Palace. Gainer had remodeled it and now showed classic movies like *Out of the Past* with Robert Mitchum, *The Flame and the Arrow* with Burt Lancaster, and *Singin' in the Rain* with Gene Kelly.

"It's a great place," Stanley said. "What was the problem?"

"The rumor was that Gainer was going to make it into a multiplex. You know what that is?"

Stanley said that he knew.

"It's one of those places where they cut the theater up and make a bunch of little cracker-box theaters out of it," Goob explained, as if Stanley hadn't spoken. "Ruins the whole thing if you ask me."

Stanley agreed. He hadn't been to see a recent movie at a multiplex in years. And he didn't intend to go anytime soon.

"Anyway," Uncle Martin went on, "Al Walker raised a big stink about it. Got a lot of people together and marched on the theater. They had picket signs and everything. He and Gainer got into a little tussle about it. Gainer got a bloody nose out of it. Turned out it was all just a big misunderstanding, but it was hectic there for a while."

So Al Walker would resort to violence in defense of the past. It wasn't exactly a shooting, but it was suggestive. Stanley added it to his file of information.

He asked Uncle Martin and Goob if they'd like to take in a movie at the Palace some night.

"We might," Goob said. "You gonna get us dates?"

"I'll see what I can do," Stanley said.

⤚ 27 ⤙

When No Birds Sing

Stanley would have liked to stay in town and talk to Al Walker and maybe even Burl Cabot, but it was getting late. He wanted to be back at the inn when Marilyn arrived.

Bill Caldwell met him at the door. "You got a phone call from that Dresser fella, the one that used to be on the radio? He said to tell you that Grant Tyler wasn't in the Big Apple. He said you'd know what that meant. Do you?"

Stanley wasn't sure. It could mean that Grant was in Higgins taking potshots at Burl Cabot. It could also mean that he was actually in New York but that Troy just couldn't locate him.

Stanley thanked Bill for the message and asked about his guests, all of whom were still out sight-seeing. Then he checked on the cats. Sheba and Binky were in their baskets. Cosmo was in the utility room, eating. Stanley topped off their water bowls and went out front to wait for Marilyn.

While he waited, he sat on the porch and looked at the late-afternoon sky, which was turning a nice shade of reddish orange. That was supposed to mean fair weather, but you could never tell about those old weather sayings. Sometimes they were way off the mark. It made a pleasant sight, however.

After ten or fifteen minutes, Marilyn's police cruiser pulled into the front yard. Stanley greeted her as she got out of the car.

He said, "I thought I'd show you some of the places where the car tore up the grass. You'll see that it wasn't just joyriders."

He led Marilyn around in back of the inn and pointed out several spots where huge chunks of soil had been ripped up by the car's back tires.

"The car didn't leave any clear tracks, though, Stanley," Marilyn pointed out. "It just tore hunks of the ground and flattened your grass pretty badly. There's no question that someone was here, but the truth of the matter is that joyriders could have done all that. It wouldn't be out of the ordinary at all."

She sounded skeptical, and Stanley tried to think of some way to prove that he was right and Kunkel was wrong.

"It wasn't some joyrider who hit me in the head," he said. "It was someone big, really big. It could easily have been the same person who took a shot at Burl Cabot today."

"I suppose that's possible," Marilyn said, but she still didn't sound convinced. "Where were you when you got hit?"

"That happened back in the trees. Maybe something fell out of the car when that big guy got out, some kind of clue. We could at least look."

Marilyn agreed and they walked back toward the creek. When they were among the trees and not far from the creek, Stanley looked over his shoulder at the inn. No one was in sight, and he wasn't likely to get Marilyn in a more private place. The shadows were deepening among the pines, and birds were singing somewhere nearby.

"There's something we need to talk about."

Marilyn looked at him and smiled. "Joyriders?"

"No. Brad Bridger."

It might have been nothing more than Stanley's imagination, but he thought that for just a fraction of a second, Marilyn looked guilty.

"What about Brad?"

"It's not just about him. It's about the two of you. And the two of us."

For the first time since he'd come back to Higgins, Stanley was treated to the sight of Marilyn blushing, if only slightly.

"What about the two of us?"

Stanley knew what he wanted to say, but he didn't know exactly how to put it into words. He worked better with at least a brief rehearsal. Not to mention a script. But he knew that he had to try.

"Well, uh, I've been hearing things."

It wasn't a great beginning, he had to admit. Marilyn put her hands on her hips and looked up at him.

"What kind of things?"

This wasn't going the way Stanley had thought it would. It would have been much easier if Marilyn would simply admit that she'd been seeing Bridger, beg Stanley's forgiveness, and say she'd never do it again. He'd known it wouldn't be that easy, but somehow he'd kept hoping that it might be.

"Well?"

Stanley tried again. "People say you've been going out with him. With Brad."

"What people?"

"Just about everyone I've talked to lately. It seems that I'm the only one who didn't know."

"And you believed these people?"

"I didn't want to, but they seemed pretty positive. That's why I thought I'd mention it to you."

Marilyn took a deep breath, let it out, and relaxed. "It's true."

"I was afraid you'd say that."

Marilyn reached out to touch his arm. "It's like this, Stanley. When you moved back here, I realized that I was attracted to you. I sort of let you know it, and things took their natural course."

Stanley smiled. "They sure did. And I enjoyed it. I thought you enjoyed it, too."

"I did. But then along came Brad." She paused. "Well, that's not exactly right. He didn't just come along. He was around all the time. But he was a coworker, and I didn't pay much attention to him. He's a good bit younger than I am, after all."

"Not that much younger."

"But younger. I didn't know that he had any interest in me. It wasn't until after I started going out with you that he let me know he did."

"Why did he wait so long?"

"He said that he didn't want to rush into anything. He wanted me to get over my husband's death. I thought that was sweet."

Stanley didn't think it was sweet. He thought it was a line. But he didn't say so.

"You could have told me."

"I know. And I was going to. I've only been out with him a couple of times, and I told myself that I'd tell you when the right opportunity presented itself. I guess I forgot how people talk in a small town like this. I should have known you'd find out. I didn't want it to be like this, Stanley."

"Me neither."

"But that's not to say that I like Brad any more than I do you. Or even as much. I was flattered when he asked me out, but I got over that. He's fun to be with, but so are you. I don't want to lose you, Stanley."

The woods were almost completely silent now. The birds had stopped singing for some reason or other. Stanley wondered if that might be symbolic.

"You haven't lost me," he said. "But I'm not sure I like splitting time with Brad."

"It won't be for long. I just need some time to make a decision." Marilyn looked at Stanley accusingly. "And it's not as if I'm the only one who's been seeing someone else."

"What do you mean?" Stanley asked, though he had a sinking feeling that he already knew the answer.

"I mean you and Lacy Falk."

"Uh."

"You're not the only one with spies, Stanley. And I'm the chief of police. I'm sure my spies are much better than yours. They've been in place for years."

Stanley was sure that her spies were better than his, too, but he was nevertheless amazed that Marilyn had already heard about him and Lacy. It didn't seem possible that she could have found out already. He wondered just exactly what and how much she'd heard, but he wasn't about to ask.

And he didn't have time.

Just then, the shooting started.

⌒ 28 ⌒

Flying Lead

Stanley heard the sharp sound of the first shot, and he even heard the bullet slap into a tree not three feet from him. He saw slivers of bark jump off the tree, but he still didn't quite know what was happening.

Marilyn did. "Get down, Stanley!" she shouted.

For a horrible second Stanley flashed back to a discotheque he'd visited in a weak moment in the 1970s, but then he realized that Marilyn wanted him to drop to the ground.

He didn't. He just stood there and watched her. She pulled a pistol from her purse and let the purse fall to the ground. She went into a crouch, with the pistol held in a two-handed grip. She swung it in an arc from left to right and back again, but she didn't fire.

Someone else did. Chips of bark flew again, just above Stanley's head this time. A splinter spun off the tree and stung Stanley's cheek. He put his hand to his face and felt dampness. His fingertips were spotted with red where he'd touched himself.

"Get behind a tree, Stanley."

They were standing near some pine trees at the edge of a small clearing. Stanley wasn't sure just how much cover the trees would provide.

"The trees are bigger and thicker by the creek," Stanley said. "Let's go, then."

They ran in a sort of crouch, ducking behind trees as they went. Stanley remembered having fallen the previous evening.

"Watch your step."

"I'm watching," Marilyn said, just before she fell sprawling to the ground.

She hit hard, and Stanley thought he heard something crack. "Are you okay?" he asked, bending down.

Marilyn groaned and turned over. "Help me sit up."

Stanley put his hands under her arms and lifted her into a sitting position. He leaned her against the trunk of a pine tree just before another bullet smashed into it. The sweet smell of freshly cut wood was in the air, but the bullet had struck high above their heads.

"I think I might have broken my finger. It was trapped in the trigger guard."

Her finger looked very red to Stanley. It wasn't swollen yet, but it was twisted at an odd angle.

"Does it hurt?"

"Not yet. But it will before long. You're going to have to defend us."

Stanley looked at the pistol that was lying a few feet away. He could tell it was a revolver, but that was the extent of his knowledge.

"Pick it up, Stanley."

Stanley picked it up gingerly and looked at it as if it might bite him. "Is the safety on?"

Marilyn laughed weakly. "Revolvers don't have safeties. And don't hold it between your fingers like that. It's not going to hurt you."

"Easy for you to say."

"Hold it the way I was."

Stanley tried, but the pistol felt big and awkward in his hands.

"Just wrap your left hand around the bottom fingers of your right." Marilyn watched as Stanley experimented. "That's better. It's a double-action .38. That means that all you have to do to fire it is squeeze the trigger."

"I don't want to kill anyone."

"There's probably not much danger of that, as long as you don't shoot in the direction of the inn."

"Which direction should I shoot in?"

"We'll just have to wait and see where the next shot comes from."

Stanley didn't like standing there like that. He didn't like holding the pistol. He didn't like the idea that he was going to have to shoot it.

"Grip it firmly."

Stanley tried.

"Don't let your hand shake. You don't have to grip it *that* hard. Just relax."

"Ha."

Another shot came from his right. It tore through one of the branches and a couple of pine needles drifted down.

"Fire a round in the shooter's direction, Stanley. You won't hit unless it's by accident, but you might scare him."

Stanley closed his eyes and tightened his finger on the trigger.

"Open your eyes. Otherwise you might shoot me. Or one of your trees."

Stanley didn't want to hit Marilyn. He didn't even want to hit a tree. So he opened his eyes.

"Now extend your arms. Just relax and squeeze gently."

Stanley took a deep breath. He let it out slowly, relaxed, and let his mind drift. For a second it was as if he could smell the smoke of a campfire, and he thought he saw ghostly shadows flitting through the trees. He remembered the battle that had been fought not far from where he stood and the bravery of the men who had fought in it.

The Union soldiers had been lost and running, but they had stood and fought when the time came. Two of them had died fighting.

The men from Higgins had believed they were defending their town from invaders. They hadn't asked someone else to do the job for them. They'd taken up arms and done it themselves.

Stanley came from people like that, people who didn't let anyone push them around. He couldn't let his ancestors down. For that matter, he couldn't let himself and Marilyn down.

Stanley squeezed the trigger of the pistol gently. He had no idea of what to expect, and the explosion surprised him when it came. He didn't flinch, however, and the bullet tore off for parts unknown.

"Very good, Stanley. You're a natural."

For perhaps the hundredth part of a second, Stanley allowed himself to believe Marilyn. In that brief time, he felt the way he'd felt during the reenactment, like one of those soldiers from so long ago.

"Now he knows that we can shoot back," Marilyn said. "Let's see how he responds."

The shooter responded by getting off two shots close together. More pine needles showered down.

Stanley didn't wait for Marilyn to tell him what to do. He pulled the trigger of the pistol twice. The whole area echoed with the crashing sound of gunshots, and Stanley's eyes watered in the acrid smoke.

Stanley could see Marilyn's lips moving, but he couldn't hear what she was saying. He had to ask her to repeat it.

"I said, 'Hold your fire.' You don't want to fire all your cartridges. You should have a couple left. Save them for later. You might need them."

The trees were thick around them, and Stanley had no real idea of where the shots had come from. It was late afternoon, and the shadows were deeper. Soon it would be getting dark. Stanley didn't like the idea of being trapped in the woods after dark with a crazed gunman. He mentioned that to Marilyn.

"Someone must have heard the shots," Marilyn said. "Are Bill and Caroline at the inn?"

Stanley said that they were.

"Then they'll have called my office, don't you think? It's not as if gunshots are common around here, not when there's not even a reenactment going on. Someone should be here soon."

"Who's on duty?" Stanley asked, hoping that he didn't already know the answer to his question.

But he did.

"Officer Kunkel," Marilyn said.

≋ 29 ≋

Once Is More Than Enough

Officer Kunkel arrived shortly thereafter, with what appeared to be the entire Higgins police force trailing along behind. They were followed by an ambulance and a fire truck.

Kunkel took charge, sending the other police out into the woods after officiously explaining the proper search patterns to them, dismissing the firefighters, and trying to get Marilyn into the ambulance.

Stanley didn't think the search would do much good. It was getting too dark to find anything. But he wasn't a professional, so he kept his mouth shut.

Marilyn kept telling Officer Kunkel that she had no intention of riding into town in an ambulance: "It's only my finger. I don't need an ambulance."

Brad Bridger was by her side, the very picture of solicitude. Watching him, Stanley thought about how Burl Cabot must have felt, knowing that his wife was sneaking around with Rance Wofford. He would have felt much worse than Stanley was feeling right now, which was pretty bad, but would he have been hurt enough to kill?

Burl had certainly known about his wife and Wofford. Stanley had discovered firsthand how hard it was to keep a secret in Higgins. You could keep it for a while, maybe, the way Brad and Marilyn had, but sooner or later the truth was going to come out.

"It wouldn't hurt to ride in the ambulance," Bridger told Marilyn. "You might have internal injuries."

"I fell down. What kind of internal injuries could I have?"

"Ruptured spleen," Kunkel said. "Peritonitis. Fractured ribs. Maybe gastrointestinal bleeding. You never can tell about a fall."

"I'll bet he took a class," Stanley said.

Kunkel glared at Stanley, but he addressed his question to Marilyn: "What was the cause of all this, anyway?"

"Joyriders," Stanley said.

Kunkel turned and took a step toward him, but Bridger stepped between them.

"Let's be civilized," Brad said. "There's no need for you to be spiteful, Stanley."

"If Kunkel had done his job last night, he might have caught whoever's been slinking around here," Stanley said. "He acted as if nothing had happened, even after I tried to tell him."

"I said it was joyriders," Kunkel told them. "I still think that's what it was."

"And you think they had so much fun that they came back with their guns?" Stanley asked.

"Never mind that," Bridger said. "Can't you see that Marilyn's hurt? I have to get her into town."

"You should stay here and investigate," Stanley said quickly. "I'll take her to the hospital."

"I'm not going to the hospital," Marilyn said. "I'm going to see Dr. Randall. He'll take care of my finger, and everything will be fine. I can drive myself."

Her face was pale, and she looked to Stanley to be none too steady on her feet.

"You might pass out from the pain," he said. "I'll take you."

"Oh, all right. Brad, you stay here and help with the search. Bring in anything that looks out of place. Have someone bring my car in."

Bridger didn't look pleased with his assignment, but he accepted it with good grace. He said that he'd have someone take care of the car, and then he walked off into the trees.

"Can you walk?" Stanley asked Marilyn.

"I can walk just fine. Don't worry about me. Worry about yourself."

Stanley didn't ask what she meant until they were in the car and on the way to town.

"I meant that it's beginning to look as if Rance Wofford might not have been the target after all," Marilyn said. "Taking in today's shooting along with what happened last night, it's looking more and more like someone's trying to kill you."

Stanley wasn't at all sure that was the case, but he didn't think he wanted to tell Marilyn what his theories were. She'd just tell him to stay out of the investigation.

So he said, "Now there's a comforting thought. I wonder who it could be."

"If I knew that, I'd arrest him."

Stanley thought about Duffy Weeks, who was at least pretty sure he'd killed Wofford. He certainly hadn't been shooting at Stanley.

And he thought about Grant Tyler, who'd been at the campfire the night before the shooting. He would have had no reason to kill Wofford, but he might have thought he had one to kill Stanley. And Tyler could easily enough be prowling around Higgins.

But would Tyler have taken a shot at Burl Cabot? Something about that shooting still bothered Stanley, though he couldn't quite put his finger on it.

As for Neddy Drake, he didn't like Wofford, either. Wofford had come into Neddy's place of business and tried to humiliate him in front of his customers. That wasn't a nice thing to do, but Neddy didn't seem upset enough to try to kill Wofford for it. And Neddy had nothing against Stanley, not that Stanley was aware of, at least.

And finally there was Al Walker, who had proved once in the past that he was willing to fight to preserve the heritage of one of Higgins's old buildings. If Wofford had been allowed to make all the changes that people had been hinting at to Stanley, he could have significantly altered the face of the town. Walker wouldn't have liked that, but how angry would it have made him, really? Stanley didn't know because he hadn't yet had a chance to talk with him.

"You're awfully quiet, Stanley," Marilyn said. "What are you thinking about?"

"Nothing much. I was just wondering who might dislike me enough to shoot me. Not counting Brad Bridger, that is."

"Surely you don't suspect Brad. He's on the police force, Stanley. He wasn't anywhere near the inn when the shooting started."

"How do you know?"

"I . . . well, I just know."

"Would you mind checking?" Stanley said, hoping that Brad hadn't been out somewhere with Marilyn.

"I don't mind checking. I really can't believe you're this jealous, Stanley."

"How jealous do you think I am?"

"Jealous enough to accuse Brad of trying to kill you." Marilyn smiled. "I suppose I should be flattered."

"I wish you would be. And I wish you'd forget about Brad. I don't like being jealous."

"What if I told you that I was a little bit jealous, too?"

"Who of?"

"Lacy Falk."

Stanley started to say that Marilyn had nothing to be jealous about, but then he realized that might not be precisely true. He *had* kissed Lacy, after all. And he'd even enjoyed it.

He found himself wondering if Marilyn had ever kissed Brad Bridger, and the thought upset him more than he'd thought it would.

"Watch the road, Stanley! You almost swerved right off."

"I guess I'm still a little upset about what just happened. It's not every day that someone takes a shot at me."

"It's getting to be a lot more common than it should be."

"Maybe it won't happen again," Stanley said, but he had a horrible feeling that it would.

For many years I was self-appointed inspector of snowstorms and rainstorms, and did my duty faithfully, though I never received one cent for it.

—Thoreau, *Journal,* February 22 [1846?]

Rain, rain, go away,
Come again some other day.

—Nursery rhyme

⌒ 30 ⌒

Anyone Home?

Stanley went into Dr. Randall's office with Marilyn and stayed to watch the doctor set her finger. Randall gave her something for the pain, and Marilyn didn't even flinch when Randall straightened the finger. Stanley wondered if he could be that brave. He didn't think so. He didn't know for certain, of course, never having broken a finger, but he was pretty sure that he didn't have a high threshold for pain, medication or not.

After the finger was set and splinted, Marilyn asked Stanley for a ride to the police station, and he was glad to oblige.

"I'd like to take you to a movie this weekend," he said as they drove. "At the Palace. Gainer's showing *Bride of Frankenstein*, the restored print. There's nothing like great black-and-white photography. It's supposed to be gorgeous."

"I'd like to go. What about Brad?"

Stanley felt a twinge of dismay. "You mean you want him to come along with us?"

"Of course not, you idiot. I mean, will it bother you if I'm still going out with him?"

"Not if it won't bother you when I go out with Lacy."

"That's not fair."

"You know what they say: All's fair—

"—in love and war. You're right, Stanley. We can't have one set of rules for me and another set for you. I'd love to go to the movie."

"You don't happen to have a couple of older friends, do you?"

Marilyn looked at him quizzically.

"I sort of promised Uncle Martin and Goob that I'd get dates for them."

"You mean we'd be triple-dating?"

"I know, I know. It's not nearly as glamorous and romantic as the kind of evening you'd have with Brad."

"You never can tell. It might be fun. I'll see what I can do."

Stanley dropped her off at the police station, then drove back to the inn, where he had a supper of tossed salad, hush puppies, and catfish stew.

The Skidmores, who had arrived just as the police called off their search for the night, joined him. Mrs. Skidmore said that this was turning into an exciting honeymoon.

"Is it always so exciting around here?" she asked.

Stanley assured them that it wasn't and said that he hoped the rest of the evening would be peaceful.

"Oh, I hope not," Mrs. Skidmore said. "I'm beginning to expect the police to show up at any moment. You certainly do lead a thrilling life, Mr. Waters."

He told her to call him Stanley. "And it's a little too thrilling if you ask me."

"Are you going to tell us what happened?"

Stanley said that he couldn't. He had to go into town to see a friend.

Mrs. Skidmore was plainly disappointed. "Maybe we could talk when you come back."

"We'll see," Stanley said.

Duffy Weeks lived on a quiet residential street in a house that had been built sometime early in the century, probably early in the 1920s. It had a wide front porch, high ceilings, and windows all around.

Stanley parked in front and looked at the house. The porch light wasn't on, but a light was on in one of the back rooms. Stanley got out of his car and walked up on the concrete porch. The night was cool, and a faint smell of smoke was in the air, as if someone might be rushing the season with a fire on the grate.

There was no doorbell at the front door, just a corroded brass knocker. There was no answer to Stanley's knock. He knocked again, and again there was no answer.

Since the light was in the back of the house, Stanley followed the porch around to a side door. There was no knocker there, so he rapped on the facing with his knuckles.

No one came to open the door. There was no movement in the house at all as far as Stanley could tell.

He tried to peer in through the top half of the door, but it was made of pebbled glass and he could see nothing inside the house. He knocked again, and while he was knocking with his left hand, he tried the doorknob with his right.

The doorknob turned easily, and the door swung inward for about an inch before Stanley stopped its momentum.

"Duffy?" he called through the crack. "It's me. Stanley Waters."

Duffy didn't answer. Stanley thought about going inside the house, but he was hesitant. He'd been shot, chased by someone in a black car, hit in the head by that same someone, and then shot at again. It might not be a good idea for someone with a run of luck like that just to walk right into a seemingly empty house. You never knew who might be lurking just inside the door.

Then Stanley thought about all the mystery novels he had read and all the movies he had seen. In them, certain things always seemed to happen in exactly the same way.

For example, if an older cop had one more day on the job before his retirement, that older cop was as good as dead.

And if someone told the private eye that he had information about a case that he couldn't reveal until later, and if that person set up a meeting with the private eye, then that person was absolutely certain to be dead when the private eye arrived at the meeting.

All of which meant that if life was imitating art, Duffy was lying on the floor inside his house, most likely in the kitchen, in a pool of blood with a knife stuck in his heart.

Or a bullet hole in his chest.

Stanley wondered whether to call the police. All he had to do was think of two words—Officer Kunkel—to discard that notion.

And, after all, this was Higgins, Virginia, not some seedy version of Los Angeles or New York City. Duffy was probably watching TV with the volume turned up high. That would explain why he hadn't heard Stanley's knock.

Of course, it didn't explain why Stanley, with the door open about two inches now, couldn't hear any sound at all from inside the house.

No TV.

No music.

No nothing.

Stanley pushed the door all the way open. The hinges squeaked, but only a little. Otherwise there was not the slightest sound except for the shushing of tires on the street as a car drove slowly past.

"Duffy? This is Stanley Waters. You told me to come by, remember?"

Stanley's voice echoed hollowly through the house.

Stanley felt a slight chill along his arms. He told himself that he was being silly and walked through the door. Duffy was in there somewhere, reading a book or the newspaper and not thinking at all about Stanley's visit. They would both have a good laugh about it when Stanley walked in on him.

The room in which Stanley found himself was a bedroom. It smelled a little strange, as if Duffy hadn't changed his sheets in too long a time. There wasn't much light in the room, but Stanley could see that the bed hadn't been made that day. And probably not in a lot longer than that.

Light was coming from Stanley's left, so he turned and walked through the bedroom, past a dresser with a tall mirror, and into a hallway. The floor creaked when he stepped into the hall, but nothing moved and there was no answering sound from elsewhere in the house.

Stanley hesitated. From where he stood in the hall, he could see into the kitchen, which was where the light was burning. He saw a white cooking range and part of a wooden breakfast table. The floor was covered with old yellow vinyl, and Stanley could see that it was peeling back along one of the seams.

He wasn't at all sure he wanted to go into the kitchen. Scenes from old movies played themselves out in his mind. None of them was pleasant. Several of them depicted a private eye getting conked on the head by an assailant who was hiding just inside the doorway.

Stanley wondered what Marilyn would think if she knew where he was and what he was doing. She would probably think that he had absolutely no business being there. At the moment, Stanley would have been inclined to agree with her.

But he didn't see how he could turn back now. If he did, he'd always wonder whether he did so because it was the right thing to do, because it was what Marilyn would expect him to do, or because he was afraid.

Telling himself that he wasn't afraid, not in the least, he stepped into the kitchen.

Duffy Weeks was there. He was lying on the floor between the breakfast table and an old white refrigerator, and he wasn't moving at all.

⫷ 31 ⫸

A True Confession

Stanley didn't move either, not for several seconds. He just stood there, looking at Duffy, who was sprawled on his back, his left arm flung out from his side, his right arm doubled under his body.

"Damn!" It was about the strongest language that Stanley allowed himself, but it was heartfelt.

On the table there was a bottle of Jack Daniel's Black Label. Beside it there was a glass, and beside the glass there was a piece of paper. There was also a short yellow pencil, but it had rolled across the table to lie on the other side.

"Suicide note," Stanley said aloud.

But maybe not a legitimate one, he thought. He knew that sometimes in the movies a killer would force his victim to write a note, then do away with him.

Stanley knew that he shouldn't touch the note, so he walked over to the table and started reading it without picking it up.

It said, "I, Harold Weeks, being of sound mind, do hereby confess that I killed Rance Wofford by shooting him in the head with my rifle."

The note was signed "Harold Weeks" in a shaky hand. Under the signature was the current date.

"Damn!" Stanley said again.

He looked down at Duffy. There was no sign of a suicide weapon. If Duffy had been murdered, the killer had made a rookie mistake and taken the weapon with him.

But then Stanley realized that if Duffy had committed suicide, the weapon might be under the body. He looked down at Duffy again.

And was amazed to see the slight rise and fall of Duffy's chest.

Stanley knelt down beside Duffy, putting a hand on his wrist to see if there was a pulse. There was, though it didn't seem to Stanley to be as strong as it should have been.

Stanley breathed deeply in relief to find any pulse at all and, in doing so, inhaled enough alcohol fumes to stagger a smaller man. The entire contents of the bottle on the table must have been transferred into Duffy's stomach.

Stanley raised Duffy's head off the floor. He slapped Duffy's cheeks gently. He would have liked to slap them much harder to punish him for the scare he'd received, but he knew it wouldn't do Duffy any good.

"Duffy," Stanley said, shaking him gently. "Wake up, Duffy, you good-for-nothing rat. You scared me to death. Come on, Duffy. Wake up."

Duffy snorted, shook his head, and emitted either a snore or a quite good imitation of a hog at the trough at feeding time. Stanley laid Duffy's head back on the floor and stood up.

Four wooden chairs were at the table. Stanley bent down, got his hands under Duffy's armpits, and dragged him upright. Then he leaned him against the refrigerator door while he hooked one of the chairs with his foot. He pulled the chair into position approximately behind Duffy, then turned Duffy's back to it and lowered him to the seat.

Duffy slumped back, and Stanley pinned him to the chair with one hand while he looked around the kitchen for a coffeemaker. He spotted it on a counter by the sink.

"Where do you keep the coffee, Duffy?" he asked, but Duffy declined to answer.

Still holding Duffy to the chair with one hand, Stanley opened the freezer compartment of the refrigerator. Inside there was one package of ground meat still wrapped in the Styrofoam and plastic it had been in at the store, a bag of frozen corn, and a can of Yuban coffee.

To reach the coffee, Stanley had to let go of Duffy, who began to slide slowly off the chair. Stanley caught him just in time, juggling the coffee in his other hand.

"You're going to have to stay put," Stanley told Duffy. "Otherwise I can't make the coffee."

Duffy, who gave no indication at all that he had heard a word, was as limp as a nylon rope.

Stanley set the coffee on the table and said, "Oh, well. Forget the coffee. If I could get you to drink it, I'd probably just have a wide-awake drunk on my hands."

He had passed a bathroom in the hall, so he pulled Duffy off the chair and across the kitchen, with Duffy's heels dragging on the floor.

The bathroom was dark. Stanley held Duffy up with one hand and flipped on the light. The floor was white tile, the bathtub was white, and so were the sink and toilet. For a second, Stanley's eyes were dazzled.

He looked at the tub. There was no shower, but there was a rubber hose with a spray attachment affixed to the faucet. Stanley dragged Duffy over to the tub and hoisted him over the side.

It wasn't easy getting Duffy inside the tub; the tub was old and the sides were high. Stanley was panting when the job was done.

And Duffy was still wearing all his clothing. Stanley decided not to worry about that. Getting the clothes off would have required more effort than Stanley was willing to expend, and it would have forced him to look at Duffy in his underwear, a sight that Stanley wanted to spare himself.

He did, however, remove Duffy's shoes. It was the least he could do. He didn't bother with the socks.

With Duffy lying peacefully on the hard, cold bottom of the tub, his head propped up against the back end, Stanley picked up the spray attachment and turned on the cold-water tap.

The water came hissing out, and Stanley directed it into Duffy's face. At first there was no reaction. Then Duffy started to twitch violently. His eyes came open; he began to cough and splutter and wave his arms. He didn't have room to do much waving, and he banged his hands on the sides of the tub. That must have hurt because he started to yell.

Or maybe he was yelling because he was wet. Stanley had kept the cold water directed on him during the spasms, and Duffy was drenched. His clothing was soaked from his shirt to his socks. He wasn't yelling anything that Stanley could understand, just meaningless noise that sounded like *arrrgggghhhhh*. Occasionally Stanley moved his hand a little too far up, and water squirted into Duffy's mouth, providing an interesting blubbery variation on the sound of the yell.

Something like two minutes passed like that, but finally Duffy seemed to figure out what was going on. He struggled to sit up, but he kept slipping back down in the tub.

Stanley kept spraying him.

Duffy coughed and started to vomit.

"Damn," Stanley said, directing the water to wash the vomitus off Duffy and down the drain. A nasty, sour smell filled the room. "You're more trouble than you're worth, Duffy."

"Arrggggghhhhhh," Duffy replied. But at least he stopped heaving.

Stanley kept spraying, and gradually Duffy's yelling became a little more coherent. After another thirty seconds or so, Stanley started to get an idea of what Duffy was saying. It wasn't very gracious, so Stanley decided to ignore it and keep on spraying water.

Another half a minute passed. Duffy managed to get a grip on the sides of the tub and push himself into a sitting position. This time he didn't slide back down.

Stanley figured it was about time to turn off the water, so he did.

"Jesus, Stanley. Were you trying to drown me?"

"No. Just sober you up."

"I think you did. Partially. I can't say that I feel very good, though."

"No wonder. How much of that bottle of Jack Daniel's did you drink?"

Duffy shuddered. "All of it."

"I thought you might have."

Duffy's teeth started to chatter. "I'm c-c-cold, S-Stanley. How about a towel?"

There was a towel rack by the tub, and Stanley handed Duffy the none-too-clean towel that was hanging there.

Duffy rubbed his hair and face for a while and then stood up. He was a little wobbly, and he put a hand against the wall to steady himself. After a few seconds he was able to step out of the tub onto the bath mat.

"There're some more towels in that closet." Duffy pointed to a built-in cabinet by the sink.

Stanley got out another towel, a fairly clean one, and tossed it to Duffy.

"I'm going to take off these wet clothes. You want to wait outside?"

"Only if you promise not to hurt yourself."

"I'll be careful. Would you mind getting me some under-wear out of the dresser in my bedroom?"

Stanley said that he wouldn't mind.

"It's in the top drawer."

Stanley went out and found the underwear. He opened the bathroom door and tossed the underwear in to Duffy, who thanked him and said, "You can wait in the kitchen. I'll get dressed and come in there."

"Are you going to tell me about the confession?"

"Yeah, I'll tell you all about it if you'll promise to do something for me."

"What?"

"Take me to the police station. And turn me in."

32

Coffee Break

Duffy's graying brown hair was dark from the water, and he'd slicked it down on his head without drying it. Dark circles were under his red-rimmed eyes, and he looked a little like a silent-movie villain as he sat across the table from Stanley, who was holding the confession.

Stanley had made some coffee while he was waiting, and both he and Duffy had a cup in front of them. Stanley hadn't drunk much of his, but Duffy had already drunk one cup and started on another.

"I didn't really plan on passing out," Duffy said between swallows. "I thought I'd just get sort of mellow, and then when you came over, I'd give you the confession and let you drive me to the police station."

"You were mellow enough this afternoon. You certainly didn't need to drink anything else."

"Yeah, I know. I should've figured that out for myself. But I've been overdoing that sort of thing a lot lately. It was all Rance Wofford's fault."

"Are you ready to tell me about that?"

Duffy took a big swallow of coffee, swallowed, and looked

down at his saucer as if the answer to Stanley's question might be written there. Apparently it wasn't.

"I don't know whether I can or not."

"Just give it a try. You can stop anytime you want."

Duffy set his coffee cup in the saucer and pushed it away from him.

"It started a few months ago. Right after I told Wofford that there was no way I was going to sell him the bar. I don't know whether you know it or not, Stanley, but Wofford was trying to buy up nearly everything in town."

"I heard about it."

"I think he was just greedy. He came here, he started buying places, and he just couldn't stop."

Stanley knew there were people like that, people who were obsessed with owning things, but he thought there was more to Wofford's problem than that. Wofford seemed also to want to make money from what he owned. He would buy the properties, and then he'd find out a way to make more money from them than the previous owners had been doing. If he had to change the whole face of the town to do it, it wouldn't matter to him. He hadn't been born in Higgins. He hadn't even lived there for long. Even if he knew something about the town's history and heritage, he wouldn't have cared about it.

Of course, he'd had no problem in joining the reenactment group, but it was all probably just a game to him, or just a history lesson with no meaning beyond that. It wouldn't have been what it was to the others, an exercise in recapturing a living past that had an intimate connection with the living present.

"I didn't want to sell him my place," Duffy said. "It's about all I have in the world."

Stanley thought about that and realized it was true. As far as Stanley knew, Duffy didn't have any family living in Higgins, and the people who were part of the reenactment group were more like acquaintances than close friends. Duffy had never married, so he didn't have a wife or children. Most of the time he kept to himself, whether he was at work or at home.

"I'm sure Rance must have understood your reasons for not

wanting to sell. I'll bet they didn't make any difference to him, though."

"They sure didn't. So he went looking for a way to force me to give him what he wanted."

Duffy got up, went to the coffeemaker, and poured some more of the dark brown liquid from the carafe. He came back to the table and drank several swallows before continuing.

"He found a way, Stanley."

Stanley waited. He figured that Duffy would tell him eventually just exactly what way Wofford had found.

It took a while. Duffy drank another entire cup of coffee without speaking before he finally decided to finish his story.

He set down the cup, looked across the table at a point about six inches above Stanley's head, and said, "I'm gay, Stanley."

Stanley waited a while longer, thinking that surely there had to be more to Duffy's story than that. But as it turned out, there wasn't.

Finally Stanley said, "That's it? That's the whole thing? That you're gay?"

Duffy didn't meet Stanley's eyes. "That's it."

"You don't molest children or guys in public toilets, do you?"

Duffy's head jerked up. "Are you crazy? Of course I don't molest children or guys in public toilets. I don't molest anyone. That's a terrible thing to say."

"I apologize. But, the way you were talking, I thought you were guilty of something terrible."

"I'm not guilty of anything. It's just the way I am."

"So what are you worried about?"

"You don't understand. You don't know what it's like to hide what you are for forty years and then to have someone threaten to expose you."

"You're right about that. I wore a toupee to hide my bald head for a while, but that's about it."

Duffy was getting upset. "This isn't funny, Stanley."

"I didn't mean to imply that it was. But just listen to yourself, Duffy. You're acting as if being gay was some sort of crime. There are openly gay actors in TV these days with their own sitcoms. What's the big deal?"

"We aren't on TV. We're in Virginia."

"Well, there's that."

"Yeah. And you can imagine what would happen to me and my business if everyone found out."

"Probably nothing. I think you're overreacting, Duffy."

"You don't know a thing about it. I've kept a big part of my life a secret for forty years, and I can't stand to think what people would say about me if they found out the truth. Wofford was going to tell them, no question. He hired a detective to do the dirty work, and he had the goods on me. That's why I've been drinking too much lately, I guess."

"You're telling the truth to me."

"That's because I think you can keep a secret. And I thought you'd find out anyway. Everyone knows how you solved Belinda's murder. They talk about it all the time. You found out things that the police would never have figured."

Stanley was flattered. He'd enjoyed his little fling at investigation, and he liked the idea that others appreciated what he'd done. At the same time, he thought they were giving him far too much credit.

"The police would have found out in a little while," Stanley said. "I just sped up the process."

"Maybe so, but I don't think so. I knew you'd find out about me. Rance Wofford did, and you would have, too. I just wanted to get it over with. I don't think you'll tell anyone, and I wanted you to know why I killed Wofford. I'm not sorry, you know."

"I thought you weren't sure you killed him."

"I'm sure now. I've thought about it a lot, and I know I must have done it. I may not remember doing it, for sure, but I did it, and I want to take my punishment."

"What are you going to tell the police?"

"I'll tell them that I killed him because he was pressuring me and because he was a jerk. Both those things are true. Besides, they won't care much about a motive as long as they have my confession. Now are you going to take me in, or not?"

"What about your bar?"

"I talked to Dale Tobler this afternoon. He's my evening bartender, and he's been wanting to buy the place for a long time.

I'm going to sell it to him. I killed Wofford to keep it, and now I'm selling it. That's called irony, I guess."

Stanley said that he guessed so, too.

"Anyway, you don't have to worry about me. Everything's taken care of. If you don't want to drive me to the jail, that's all right. I thought it might be easier if I had someone to go with me, but I can go by myself."

"I'll go with you. But you'll have to answer a couple of questions for me first."

"What questions?"

"Did you try to run me down with a car last night?"

"Are you kidding?"

"No."

"Well, I didn't."

"All right. Did you take a shot at Burl Cabot earlier today?"

"Me? Take a shot at Burl? Why would I do that?"

"That's what I'd like to know. Did you?"

"No."

"Just one more question, then, speaking of taking shots at people. Did you shoot at me and Chief Tunney late this afternoon?"

"I was too drunk to shoot at anyone late this afternoon. Why are you asking me this stuff, Stanley?"

"Because I'm curious."

"Are you satisfied now?"

"No, but I'll take you to the police station if that's really what you want me to do."

"That's really what I want you to do."

Stanley stood up. "All right, then. Let's go."

33

He's in the Jailhouse Now

It all took a while.

Stanley called Marilyn, who wasn't at home. He didn't want to think about where she might be or whether it involved Brad Bridger. So he called the night dispatcher, Geraldine Calloway, who said that she'd page Marilyn.

"Tell her I'm bringing in a prisoner," Stanley said. "Someone who claims to have shot Rance Wofford."

"Who is it?"

"Duffy Weeks."

"Well, I'll be damned. How long will it take you to get here?"

"Five minutes."

After that, Stanley drove Duffy to the police station. Marilyn came in, and Stanley and Duffy went into her office.

Marilyn was upset, and Stanley's asking about her finger didn't cheer her up any. Stanley told her with a perfectly straight face and without turning red that he hadn't been investigating anything and that Duffy had called him because he wanted to confess to someone.

"You should have called me," Marilyn said harshly to Duffy, taking some of her anger out on him.

"Stanley's a friend," Duffy said. "I wanted him to bring me in. It was easier that way. I have a signed confession for you."

He took the confession out of his shirt pocket, unfolded it, and handed it across the desk to Marilyn.

She didn't take it. "Don't give me that yet. I have to read you your rights first."

She took a card from her purse and read Duffy the Miranda rights. He listened patiently until she was finished and then handed her the confession. She took it this time, read it, and put it down among all the other papers on her desk.

"You're not making this up, are you? This isn't some kind of gag you've worked out with Stanley?"

"That really hurts, Marilyn," Stanley said. "Of course it's not some kind of gag. Duffy really believes that he shot Rance Wofford."

Marilyn gave Stanley a shrewd look. "What do you mean by saying that Duffy 'really believes' it. Don't you believe it?"

"I'm not sure. He might have done it, but there are a lot of loose ends. I'm sure you know what all of them are."

"I know, all right," Marilyn said, and she then asked Duffy the same questions that Stanley had asked him earlier in his kitchen.

Duffy gave her the same answers he'd given Stanley.

"I don't know why you're asking me those things," he said when he'd finished answering. "I shot Wofford, and that's all there is to it. I'm willing to admit that, but I didn't do any of those other things, and you can't make me say that I did."

"I don't want you to say that you did," Marilyn told him. "I just want to make sure that you didn't."

"Well, I didn't. You can believe that. Ask Stanley about my condition this afternoon. I couldn't have shot at anyone."

"He's telling the truth about that," Stanley said. "It might have been possible for him to shoot at Burl this morning, but he didn't do anything of the kind late this afternoon. And if he didn't, who did?"

"That's what I'd like to know," Marilyn said.

"Maybe there's more to this than just Rance Wofford," Stanley suggested.

"I tried to tell you that this afternoon," Marilyn said. "It could be that someone's after you."

"I'm not after him," Duffy said. "I was just after Rance Wofford, and now that he's dead, I'm satisfied. I don't want to kill Stanley. Stanley's okay."

"So you weren't trying to kill Stanley when Rance Wofford stepped in the way?"

"Good grief," Duffy said. "Let me explain what happened."

He told Marilyn about being a little drunk the night before the shooting and about how everyone thought it would be a hoot to fire their rifles at Rance Wofford.

"Of course the rifles weren't supposed to be loaded," he said. "But mine was. I don't know how it got loaded, but that's because *I* was loaded."

"It's good that you can joke about this, Duffy," Marilyn said. "But it's not a joking matter."

"Sorry about that. I couldn't resist. Besides, it's the truth."

Marilyn cocked an eyebrow. "Are you going for some kind of diminished-responsibility plea?"

"Why should I do that? I killed the guy, he deserved killing, and I'm not one bit sorry that he's dead. I'm willing to take full responsibility for my actions."

"Very public-spirited of you," Stanley said. "It's too bad that more criminals don't feel the same way."

Marilyn gave Stanley a warning glance. "Didn't you hear me tell Duffy that this wasn't a joking matter, Stanley? You and Duffy must think this is the *Original Amateur Hour*."

"I remember that show," Duffy said. "I'm surprised that you do, though. I didn't think you were that old."

"Never mind," Marilyn said. "You won't think it's so funny when you're locked up."

Duffy frowned. "I probably won't, will I."

"No," Stanley said. "It's not exactly Club Med."

Marilyn stood up. "We're going to have to book you, Duffy.

Then we'll see that you get a nice cell. Stanley, you've been a big help, but I think you'd better go home now."

"Sure." Stanley shook hands with Duffy, told him good-bye, and left the station.

But he didn't go home.

❧ 34 ❧

Gene, Gene, the Dancing Machine

After leaving the police station, Stanley drove straight to Al Walker's house, which was located in the middle of a tree-lined block not that far from Duffy's home.

During the short drive, Stanley noticed that a black car seemed to be following him. It didn't look a thing like the car that had chased him on the previous evening, so he didn't think too much about it. He parked at the curb in front of Walker's house. Lights were on in several rooms, so Stanley got out and went up to the door. Walker had a doorbell, and Stanley rang it.

The door was opened almost immediately by a boy wearing a faded *Lost World* T-shirt and jeans. He looked to Stanley to be about seven or eight years old, but Stanley wasn't good at guessing children's ages.

The boy looked up at Stanley and said, "Who are you?"

"I'm Stanley Waters. Who are you?"

"Gene." He did a fancy dance step with a twirl and a dip. "Are you the guy that got shot?"

"That's right. Are you a dancer?"

"I'm a dancing machine. Can I look at your head?"

Stanley sighed and bent over.

"Cool. How many stitches do you have?"

"I don't know. Is your father at home?"

A male voice called from inside the house, "Gene, is someone at the door?"

Gene turned around and said, "Yeah. It's Mr. Waters. He's showing me his head."

Al Walker came into the room and stood behind Gene. Walker was short, stout, and red-faced. His hair was cut short, a crew cut.

"Hey, Stanley," Walker said, opening the door wider. "Come on in."

Gene danced out of the way, but he managed to stay close to the door.

"Donna and I were cleaning up in the kitchen," Walker said. "What can I do for you, Stanley?"

"I need to talk to you, Al." Stanley looked meaningfully at Gene. "In private."

Al patted his son on the head and said, "Gene, you go help your mom with the dishes. I have to talk to Mr. Waters."

"Aw, Dad, you never let me hear the good stuff."

"This is just business," Stanley said. "Very boring."

"That's what Dad always says. But I don't think so."

"Go on, Gene. If there's anything exciting to tell, I'll let you know later."

"You always say that, too," Gene said, but he left the room, executing a fancy dance step or two that spun him around twice as he crossed the rug.

"Have a seat, Stanley," Walker said when Gene was safely out of earshot.

The room was a small den, with a couch, several chairs, and a TV set against one wall. Stanley sat in one of the chairs, a platform rocker, and Walker sat on the couch.

"Now, what brings you here? I'll bet you didn't come to discuss how my math classes went today."

"I hope they went okay, but that's not why I'm here. I came to tell you something that no one else knows. Duffy Weeks confessed to killing Rance Wofford."

Walker sat forward on the couch. "Why would he do that?"

"Because he thinks he did it. But he told me that all of you were talking about it the night before it happened."

"Now wait just a minute. If you're trying to imply—"

"I'm not implying a thing. I'm just stating a fact."

Walker relaxed slightly. "All right. I guess I'm being too touchy. We did talk about it, but that doesn't mean that any of the rest of us had anything to do with shooting Wofford. Talking's not doing. We'd had a little to drink, 'shine if you want to know the truth. It's more authentic than, say, beer. And it can make you say things."

Stanley wasn't a connoisseur of moonshine, but he'd had a sip or two. Right out of the mason jar. It was generally potent enough to loosen anyone's tongue, or to strip varnish if it came to that.

"Was Grant Tyler there?"

"He came around for a while. He said that he wanted to get some background for his broadcast the next morning. He seemed like an okay guy."

"Did he have anything to drink?"

"He sure did." Walker smiled at the memory. "I thought he was going to choke to death on the first one."

"And did he have anything to say when you talked about Wofford?"

Walker closed his eyes and gave it some thought. "It seems to me he said something like, 'I'd rather you shoot Stanley Waters.' He must not be one of your fans."

"He isn't. Did anyone respond to that?"

"Lacy did. She said—"

"Wait a minute. Lacy was there?"

"That's what I just said. She likes to come out and have a little touch of the 'shine now and then. We don't mind. She's fun to have around. She knows more jokes than any of the guys."

"But this is supposed to be a campfire before a battle. Women wouldn't be there."

Walker looked through the doorway that led to the kitchen, then turned back to Stanley. "We don't mind if she's there. She comes in costume."

Thinking about Lacy's costume, Stanley understood why no one minded having her around.

"What did she have to say?"

"She said that she hoped no one would shoot you. She was saving you for something special." Walker paused. "Maybe it's none of my business, Stanley, but—"

"It's probably not," Stanley said, not wanting to hear about Brad Bridger again. "Did any other women come out for the campfire?"

"Donna was there. I think she comes because Lacy does. And Betty Cabot was there, too. Burl's wife."

"I know Burl's wife. How did she react when you talked about shooting Wofford?"

"You know about her and Wofford?"

"I heard a rumor that she was going out with him. I don't know that it's true."

"Oh, it's true, all right. Or it was true."

" 'Was'?"

"Something must have happened, because she was all for shooting Wofford."

Stanley was trying to keep up with the turns the conversation was taking. It wasn't easy.

"She was?"

"In fact," Walker said, "she might have been the one who suggested that we try to shoot him, now that I think about it."

"What about Burl?"

"Burl was sort of sulking in the background. I don't think he had much to say at all."

"He didn't want to shoot Wofford?"

Walker thought about it. "I think he joined in that part of it, all right. I sort of got the impression that he and his wife must have patched things up, and now they blame Wofford for everything that happened between them."

"Speaking of blame, you didn't much like Wofford, either, did you?"

Walker sat forward again. "Why wouldn't I like him? He never did anything to me."

"But he was going to change the face of Higgins, most likely.

You wouldn't have appreciated that. And you're supposed to be a pretty good shot."

Walker didn't take offense. "I'm not supposed to be pretty good. I *am* good. And you're right. I didn't like what Wofford had in mind for the town. He was an outsider, and we thought that taking him into the Irregulars would have a good effect on him, give him an idea of what the history of this region is all about. But we were wrong. He didn't care about history. He just liked dressing up and running around in the woods."

"Is that why he wasn't at the campfire?"

"He never came to campfires. He said it was damp and cold and uncomfortable."

Wofford was quite a guy, Stanley thought. He didn't seem to have a single endearing quality. He'd had the ability to make money, but that seemed to be his only gift. Except where Betty Cabot was concerned; she must have seen something more in him. Or maybe the money was an attraction for her, too. Burl probably hadn't been getting rich selling auto parts.

"So how far would you go to keep someone like Wofford from buying up all the old buildings in town, remodeling them, and putting in franchise businesses?" Stanley asked.

"I wouldn't shoot him, if that's what you're asking."

Stanley really didn't know Al Walker very well. He seemed like a mild-mannered high school teacher, so much so that Stanley was surprised he wasn't wearing a pocket protector. He had a wife and a son in the kitchen doing the dishes together. It was almost like being in the room with Ward Cleaver. But at least once in the past, Walker had resorted to violence to make a point. Stanley reminded him of that incident.

"I learned an important lesson from that," Walker said. "Gainer threatened to file assault charges against me, and I was so scared of going to jail or paying a big fine that I apologized to him every day for two weeks. He was willing to forgive and forget, and I've never done anything like that again."

"This wasn't quite the same kind of thing."

"No. It involved killing a man. Now, I'm a *very* good shot. I could have killed Wofford, all right. But I didn't. If I learned a lesson from hitting someone, would I go so far as to shoot a man? Of course not. And that's that. Anyway, didn't you say that Duffy had confessed?"

Stanley admitted that he had.

"So it's all settled. Duffy did it, and I didn't. I don't really blame you for checking things out, Stanley. Everyone in town knows what a tenacious investigator you are. We talked about it at the campfire, in fact."

"You did?"

"Sure. We talk about a lot of things. You have quite a reputation in town."

Stanley had been pleased when Duffy said pretty much the same thing, but he wasn't so sure that he was happy about it now. He didn't mind being known as someone who'd been a big help to the police, but he didn't want to be known as some kind of meddlesome amateur detective.

"I haven't really done much," he said. "Just helped the police out a little."

"You're modest, too. That's why everyone likes you, Stanley."

Everyone, Stanley thought, except whoever it was that kept trying to kill him.

He maketh his sun to rise on the evil and on the good, and sendeth rain on the just and on the unjust.

—Matthew 5:45

The quality of mercy is not strain'd,
It droppeth as the gentle rain from heaven
Upon the place beneath . . .

—Shakespeare, *The Merchant of Venice*, 4.1.184

~ 35 ~

Out of the Night

Stanley got in his car and started home, thinking about all that Walker had said. Several things bothered him.

One was the fact that Lacy had been at the campfire. Stanley didn't like that at all. He was developing a few theories about what had happened to Wofford, and while they all involved Duffy, they also involved someone else. Just whom, Stanley didn't know, but whoever it was had been at the campfire. He was sure about that.

He didn't like what he'd heard about Grant Tyler, either. If Grant had been drinking 'shine, there was no telling what might have gone through his head. He'd made it clear to everyone that he didn't have any great affection for Stanley. Wofford was the one who'd died, but with everything that had happened since, no one could be sure that Stanley wasn't the actual target.

Stanley didn't think he was the target, however, or at least that was the hypothesis he was working on. He was also developing a theory about the attacks on him since Wofford's death. He had a lot of the pieces to the puzzle, but most of them were still scattered all over the table. Nevertheless, Stanley thought he was beginning to see a pattern.

He turned on the car radio and got a station that subscribed to "the music of your life" format. "String of Pearls" was playing, which was from a bit before Stanley's time but nevertheless a song that he enjoyed. He tapped his fingers on the steering wheel and thought about what a good time he was having.

Even the really unpleasant things that had happened to him couldn't diminish the exhilaration he felt when he was actually making progress in gathering information, sifting through it and coming up with a logical answer.

It was the same feeling he'd had when he was helping Marilyn with the investigation into Belinda's death. Stanley had always enjoyed talking to people, and something about putting all the different conversations together with what he'd seen and surmised truly pleased him.

He could easily understand why professional investigators enjoyed their work so much, and he was sorry that Marilyn didn't want him working on this case, especially now that he was making some sense of it.

Besides, if Marilyn was trying to keep him out of things for his own safety, she wasn't doing a very good job. He'd already had as many close calls as he'd had before, and this time he was supposedly on the sidelines.

He suspected that Brad Bridger had something to do with Marilyn's attitude. He could just imagine Bridger telling her that Stanley was a bumbling layman who knew nothing at all about proper police procedure and who shouldn't be allowed into a professional investigation.

If that was Bridger's thinking, Stanley had to admit, even though it galled him, then Bridger had a point. Stanley wasn't a professional, and he didn't really have any business getting involved in an official investigation. That's what the police were for, after all.

"String of Pearls" ended and Johnnie Ray began singing "Cry" as Stanley told himself that he really wasn't doing the job of the police. What he was doing was entirely different.

They were examining videotapes and looking for physical evidence and doing other things that an individual couldn't really do. Stanley, on the other hand, was just talking to people, listening to their stories, and trying to make some sense of them.

On the other hand, he thought, it certainly wouldn't hurt to look at that videotape again. He was sure that there was a part of it he hadn't seen. He'd also like to see any others that Marilyn had, and he'd like to know if she'd heard anything from the FBI lab. It was probably too soon for that, however.

Stanley, thinking about the conversations he'd had and humming along with Johnnie Ray, wasn't really concentrating on his driving, which wasn't as dangerous as it might seem to anyone who didn't live in a town the size of Higgins. After dark on the tree-lined streets, there was hardly any traffic at all. Higgins wasn't known for its rousing nightlife, and Stanley had avoided driving through the center of town where the only thing resembling a crowd might have been expected.

So what happened next came as quite a surprise.

Stanley was almost to the inn when a pair of headlights dazzled his eyes. A black car burst out of a side road to his right and headed straight for his Lexus.

Stanley hardly had time to react. He jerked the wheel hard to the left, hoping to avoid a collision by driving off the shoulder and into an open field, but it didn't work out that way. The black car slammed into the Lexus's right front fender just in front of the tire.

Metal crashed and crumpled and sparked, but Stanley didn't see or hear any of those things because his driver-side air bag exploded in his face as the car shuddered to a stop.

For once Stanley was glad that he was as big as he was. He'd heard stories about people being killed by their air bags, but they were all children or small adults. Stanley was only momentarily stunned.

The air bag deflated quickly, but Stanley just sat there. A strange ringing was in his ears, and his face felt as if it had just been slapped.

He shook his head and released his seat belt, wondering who had hit him. It was a stupid accident, and he was sure his car was ruined. The bodywork would be terribly expensive, and he was afraid the frame was bent.

But it hadn't been his fault. What kind of idiot would run

into him like that? Whoever it was, he'd better have insurance and plenty of it.

Someone was screaming and pounding on his window and trying to jerk the door of the Lexus open. Stanley turned and saw a face distorted with rage but one that he recognized immediately. It belonged to Grant Tyler.

⮜ 36 ⮞

Fists of Fury

The car door was locked, but Stanley opened it and got out. He was going to ask Tyler what he was doing there and why he'd run into his car, but he didn't get the chance because Tyler hit him in the face.

He didn't hit him hard, but he hit him in a vulnerable spot—his lip, which split open and began to bleed. Stanley was so shocked that he staggered back against his car.

"Damn."

He was cursing a lot more than usual, he thought. Maybe he should have taken Marilyn's advice and gone straight home. He touched his lip and wiped his fingers on his pants.

"What's the matter with you, Grant? Are you crazy?"

"I'll show you who's crazy, you son of a bitch." Tyler stepped up and took another wild swing at Stanley's head with his right hand.

Stanley was ready this time. He caught hold of Tyler's wrist and held on tight.

"Let go, you bastard."

"Not until you calm down."

"I'm not going to calm down, you snake."

Tyler swung again, awkwardly, with his left hand. Stanley

caught that wrist and clamped down on it. They stood there for a second, Tyler hopping around as if he were barefoot on a hot griddle and trying to jerk his wrists loose.

He was jumping so vigorously that his toupee came loose and slid forward on his head. It looked as if it were about to leap off and bite Stanley in the face.

"You wrecked my car, Grant, and now you're trying to wreck me. What did I ever do to you?"

"You're trying to take my job, you gob of spit. I know all about it, and I'm not going to give up without a fight."

Stanley was finding it hard to hold on to Tyler's wrists. They were getting sweaty and beginning to slide up and down in his hands. He was afraid that Tyler was going to slip out of his grip and start trying to hit him again.

"When people say they aren't going to give up without a fight, they don't mean a fistfight," Stanley said. "This is ridiculous. I haven't been in a fight since I was a kid."

Not unless we count last night, he thought. He knew for sure now that Grant hadn't been the person who'd attacked him the previous evening, however. Grant was too small and far too clumsy.

"If I let you go, will you promise to calm down?"

"I'm going to whip your ass."

"Then I'm not going to let go."

Stanley tightened his grip, or tried to, hoping to cause Tyler at least a little pain and possibly discourage him. Tyler wasn't easy to discourage even though he couldn't get away. But he was tricky. He stopped hopping and tried a smile.

"Okay, Stanley. You win. I'll calm down. I can see now that I made a mistake. Let me go, and I'll get back in my car and leave."

"You can't leave. We're going to report this accident to the police."

"Okay, sure. Just let me go, and we'll take care of it."

"You'll have to promise not to try to hit me again."

Tyler looked contrite. "I promise."

Stanley let go of Tyler's left wrist.

Tyler smiled at him. "See? I'm calm, Stanley. This was all a huge mistake."

Stanley let go of his right wrist.

Tyler stepped back, smiled again, and tried to hit Stanley in the face again. Stanley ducked to the side, and Tyler missed his face, hitting him in the ear.

"Ouch!" Stanley reached out and grabbed Tyler again. "You really are a good-for-nothing liar, Grant."

"Let me go, Stanley. I promise I won't hit you again."

"You won't hit me again because I'm not about to let you go. Come with me."

Stanley started dragging a squirming Tyler over to a level spot of ground. About halfway there, Tyler stopped writhing and went limp. Stanley wished a bathtub were around so he could dump Tyler in it and hose him down, the way he'd done with Duffy.

But there was no bathtub, so Stanley just let Tyler down and sat on his chest.

"I . . . can't . . . breathe."

"Sure you can. I'm not *that* heavy."

"Yes . . . you . . . are."

Stanley didn't really care at the moment. His ear was throbbing, and his cut lip was stinging. It was also starting to swell a bit, making it hard for Stanley to articulate clearly.

"You could be right about how heavy I am. I'll get up before you lose consciousness, though. I promise."

Stanley let Tyler think about that. He hoped that Tyler would remember his own promise and how he'd fulfilled it. Maybe he'd worry about whether Stanley was telling the truth.

For a while Tyler said nothing, so Stanley sat on him and listened to the steam hissing in the Lexus's radiator. Or it could have been in the radiator of the car Tyler had been driving. Stanley was too sad about what had happened to get up and check. He really liked his Lexus. He couldn't believe what Tyler had done to it.

"I want to tell you a few things, Grant. Are you listening?"

"I'm . . . listening."

"Good. First of all, I'm not after your job. I wouldn't go back into daily network television if they paid me a million dollars a show."

"That's what . . . Seinfeld . . . gets."

"You're right. And I'm no Seinfeld, so they wouldn't pay me that even if I did go back. Which I'm not going to do."

"You're . . . the one . . . they want."

"Well, they're not going to get me. I have a few ideas about how you could improve the show, though, if you'd like to listen. I'll bet that within a few weeks, the numbers will be way up, and you'll get all the credit. Do you want to hear what I have to say?"

Tyler's chest rose and fell slowly under Stanley's ample rear end. "All right. I'll listen."

"Good. But first of all, you're going to have to answer some questions. I'm going to let you sit up, but if you try to run, I'll catch you and sit on you again. Do you believe me?"

"I . . . believe you."

Stanley got a firm grip on Tyler's wrists and stood up, pulling Tyler along with him. He was expecting Tyler to make an escape attempt, but he didn't. He just went limp.

Stanley didn't care. He'd already had a little practice at dragging droopy bodies that evening, and Tyler didn't weigh quite as much as Duffy. He hauled him over to the Lexus and flopped him facedown on the hood.

Tyler lay there for a minute and then slowly turned over.

"Fix your toupee. I don't like the way it's looking at me."

Tyler raised his hands to his head and felt his fake hair. Stanley wondered what it was made of. Because of his personal interest in the subject, he'd once read an article about toupees. As he remembered it, William Shatner's was made of yak hair. Or maybe that was Lorne Greene's. Stanley wasn't sure. His own had been made of real human hair, or so he'd been told. That was another reason he'd gotten rid of it. He didn't like the idea of someone else's hair sitting on top of his head.

Tyler straightened his toupee and patted it down. "This damned thing never did stay in place like they told me it would."

"That's why you should get rid of it."

"You have to be kidding. I'm not going to have my dome

flashing in the lights the way yours does. People would laugh at me."

"Don't be in such a hurry to make a decision. Think about it for a minute. Remember what happened when I ditched my rug? Ratings went up two points in the first week."

Tyler looked thoughtful. "You're right. I'd forgotten that."

"Well, give it some thought. That's my first suggestion, and it was free. Now it's your turn."

"That lip of yours doesn't look so good. You look like a bee stung you."

"You can apologize if you want to."

"I already did."

"You didn't mean it, though."

"Oh, all right. I'm sorry I hit you. It was a mistake."

"What about my car?"

"That was a mistake, too. But don't worry. I have plenty of insurance. I was driving a rental, and I took out the supplementary stuff they always try to foist off on you."

"So you admit that this was a premeditated accident."

"What is this? Are we being filmed for *The People's Court*? Of course it was premeditated. I was mad as hell at you, Stanley."

"I didn't do anything to you."

"I know that. I said I made a mistake. I don't want to talk about it anymore. Either ask me your questions or let me get out of here."

Stanley thought about having Officer Kunkel come out and do an accident report. It didn't seem like a good idea. It would be a wonderful report, Stanley was sure, but Kunkel would ask far too many awkward questions.

So he said, "We'd be more comfortable at the inn. Why don't we drive there? You can go first. I'll follow you."

"You don't trust me, do you?"

"No. I don't."

⌒ 37 ⌒

Cheese and Crackers

Stanley's guests were all upstairs. He didn't want to disturb them, so he and Tyler sat in the kitchen to talk.

Stanley had plenty of questions, and Tyler didn't hesitate to answer them. Tyler admitted that he'd been at the campfire, that he'd made the remark about shooting Stanley, and that the others had talked seriously about shooting Rance Wofford.

"But it was harmless," he insisted. "They were all kidding. They weren't going to be using bullets, or whatever they shoot in those rifles, and they'd all had a snort or two of that forty-rod. My God, after a drink of that stuff, no one's responsible for what he says."

"Did they show you their rifles?"

They were sitting at the table, and Stanley had found some nicely aged cheddar in the refrigerator. He and Tyler had each cut a wedge of it, and they were eating it with saltine crackers. The salt on the crackers burned Stanley's split lip.

Tyler cut off a thin slice of his cheese and laid it on a cracker.

"Sure they did. They all like playing with guns. Otherwise they wouldn't be out there."

"Did they show you how to load them?"

Tyler took a bite of his cracker and cheese, chewed it slowly, and then said, "Yes. Why are you asking about that?"

"Well, it seems that you weren't around when the shooting took place. No one knows where you went or what you were doing."

Tyler ate the rest of his cracker. "Could I please have a glass of water?"

Stanley liked to keep a pitcher of cold water in the refrigerator. He got a glass and poured Tyler a drink.

"Thanks." Tyler drank a swallow and set the glass on the table. "You think I shot you, don't you?"

"I don't know. That's what I'm trying to find out."

"Well, I didn't. I did go out to try to get a little different perspective on the reenactment, but that's all. I was hoping to come up with some good insights to use when I narrated the battle the next day."

"And did you?"

Tyler reached up to pat his toupee, or maybe just to be sure it was still in place. It had slipped a little to the right, not much, but enough to be noticeable. He slid it back where it belonged.

"You're right about this damned toup. I'm going to get rid of it. We'll lead up to the big event for about a week, do some teasers, get the interest level up. That'll get the ratings headed in the right direction even before I go natural."

"Good idea. Now, what about those insights?"

"I didn't get any." Tyler took another drink of water.

He was making Stanley thirsty, so Stanley got a glass of water for himself.

"You saw something, though," Stanley said. The cool glass felt good against his lip. "Didn't you?"

Tyler shook his head. The toupee slid to the left and stayed there. He shoved it back.

"I think you did see something. Why don't you tell me?"

"I would if I'd seen anything. You don't think I'm a very sensitive guy, Stanley, but I am. I've been worrying about what happened ever since that Wofford guy was shot, and I've gone back over the whole thing again and again in my head, wondering if there was anything that I could have done. But there wasn't."

"If it's been worrying you, you must have seen something."

"No. Not like you mean. I did see that man get shot, but that's all."

"Maybe it's not. Why don't you describe the whole thing for me and let me be the judge."

So that's what Tyler did.

After Tyler had told his story, Stanley gave him the rest of his suggestions for improving *Hello, World!* Tyler admitted that some of them might even work. Then Stanley sent him on his way.

"I'd put you up here, but all the rooms are full. There's a good hotel in town, though. Rance Wofford owned it, and it's still open."

"What about our accident? Aren't you doing to call the cops?"

Stanley didn't like the way Tyler called it "our accident." As far as he was concerned, it was Tyler's accident and no one else's.

"I don't think I need to call," Stanley said. "I'll file a claim with the rental company. They've got the evidence of the wreck, and you can give them my name and the particulars when you turn in the car."

"So you trust me to tell them whose fault it was?"

"I guess I'll have to."

"All right. I'll tell them the truth. I hope there won't be any trouble about it."

Stanley hoped so, too.

⌐ 38 ⌐

See What the Boys in the Back Room Will Have

The sky was cloudy the next morning, and Stanley guessed there was about a fifty percent chance that it would be raining by afternoon. It was only a guess, but he was sure it was at least as accurate as anything the weather forecasters were predicting.

After an omelette and coffee with his guests, Stanley got in the remains of his Lexus and headed for town. A man with a wrecked car should certainly have a talk with his local auto parts dealer, shouldn't he?

Probably not, Stanley thought. He should most likely be getting estimates from a couple of body shops. But it had been his radiator, not Tyler's, that was hissing after the wreck, and he was pretty sure he needed a new one.

Not that he could install it. He didn't have any idea about how to do such a thing. But he could find out how much one would cost. He told himself that it was only logical to do so. And of course he could talk to Burl Cabot about other things if he wanted to.

First, however, he drove by Bushwhackers to see if Lacy had opened for business. She had. Plenty of people liked to get their hair cut or styled early in the day before going off to Alexandria or D.C. for a little shopping or sight-seeing.

Lacy was already in fine form, joking and even singing a little as she clipped and snipped on the thin gray locks of Teresa Evans, a small, birdlike woman who wasn't going anywhere that day but who liked to get things done and over with before time for her favorite soaps.

"Hey, Stanley," Lacy called as he walked in. "I was just talking about you. How's the head today?"

"It itches."

"That's to be expected," Teresa said. "I had a cut on my arm once, needed fifteen stitches. Those stitches itched something awful. I thought I'd go crazy before they finally came out."

"I'm not going crazy," Stanley said. "Not yet, anyway."

"How about a trim?" Lacy said. "Not that you're looking shaggy."

"I don't think so. I'd like to talk to you when you're finished with Teresa, though, if you have a few minutes."

"Hell, honey, I've got all the time in the world if it's you doing the asking."

Lacy and Teresa laughed. Stanley tried to smile and show that he was a good sport, though he didn't feel much like one.

When Teresa had paid, Lacy took Stanley's arm and led him to a back room that he hadn't known existed. It was lined with shelves covered with bottles and boxes and neatly stacked towels.

"I used to sneak back here when I needed a smoke break," Lacy said when she had closed the door.

"I didn't know you smoked."

"I don't, not anymore. I still miss it, though. I could start up again tomorrow if I let myself. I dream about it around once a month. But you didn't come here to talk about my old habits, did you?"

"No."

"Did you come to get me in the back room and feel me up?"

Stanley's face got red. "No, that's not it."

"Damn. I was kinda hoping it was. Oh, well. If you didn't come for that, you didn't." She gave Stanley a wicked grin. "Wanna do it anyway?"

The redness spread all the way across the top of Stanley's head. His ears burned.

"You got yourself a split lip there, Stanley. How'd that happen?"

"I didn't come here to talk about that, either."

"Then what in the hell *did* you come here for?"

"I wanted to ask you something about the campfire before the reenactment."

"Oh. That's a pretty boring subject, Stanley, you know that?"

"I can think of something that's not boring. Tell me more about Rance Wofford and Betty Cabot."

Lacy smiled. "What's to tell? I know one thing, though. If Rance had gotten Betty in a nice, quiet little back room like this one, he wouldn't have wasted his time asking dumb questions."

"I'm not like Wofford. I'm basically a shy person."

"You're a TV star."

"I'm not on TV anymore, and I wasn't a star even when I was on. I was just the weather guy."

Lacy took two steps toward Stanley. She was standing only about an inch away. Stanley could feel the heat coming off her body, of which he was a little more conscious than was really comfortable for him.

"I like you a lot, Stanley."

"I like you, too, Lacy, but I need to know about Betty Cabot and Rance."

"Oh, all right. I swear, you try my patience, Stanley, but I've got a lot of patience. You'll see."

Stanley was sure he would, but he didn't say so. He was afraid to say anything. So he just waited.

"According to what I heard in the shop, Betty and Rance were a hot item for a good while," Lacy said at last.

She hadn't moved away, so Stanley took a step backward.

"What are you afraid of, Stanley?"

"That I won't find out what I want to know."

"Ha! I know better than that. But I'll tell you what I know. They say the husband is always the last to know when the wife is fooling around, and Burl isn't the brightest bulb on the string. It took him just about forever. But he was really mad when he finally caught on, and he took it out on Betty, not Rance. She came in here one day for a haircut, and she'd put her makeup on extra heavy. It didn't help, though. I could tell she'd had hands laid on her."

Stanley was shocked. "I didn't think Burl was that kind of person."

Lacy shook her head impatiently. "You never know who might be 'that kind of person.' I'm not what you'd call a liberated woman, Stanley, as you may have noticed, but I have to say that men are pretty stupid about spousal abuse. The good ones, like you, never can believe anybody else would do it, but they would. Take my word for it."

Stanley wanted to ask how she could be so certain, but there was a look in her eye that he'd never seen before, and he knew that now wasn't the time to question her.

"Was Betty badly hurt?" he asked instead.

"You mean physically? She didn't have any bones broken, if that's what it takes to qualify. She didn't even have a split lip like you do. But there are other kinds of hurt, Stanley. They don't show, but they mean a lot more."

Once again, Lacy sounded as if she knew exactly what she was talking about, and once again Stanley refrained from asking how she could be so sure. There was no doubt about her certainty.

"Why didn't you tell me this before?" he asked.

"It wasn't any of your business. It's still not, and I wouldn't be telling you if I didn't think you really needed to know."

"How can you be so sure I need to know?"

"Are you kidding? You passed up a chance to make out with me, Stanley. You'd damn sure *better* need to know, or else I'd be real insulted."

Stanley smiled. "I see your point." Then he thought about Betty Cabot and the smile went away. "Did you ask her about what Burl had done?"

"No. There wasn't any need to ask. I just told her that I knew of a good place to go if she needed any help. She knew what I meant, all right, but she said that everything was fine."

"What did she mean by that?"

"How do I know? She didn't file any charges against Burl, so she could've meant that she thought she deserved what happened to her. Some women take it that way, Stanley."

"I hope she didn't."

"Well, you never can tell. That was a week or so ago. When I saw her at the campfire, she looked okay. I don't think there'd been any more trouble."

"That's good."

"Was there anything else you wanted to know?"

Stanley told her that there wasn't.

"All right, then. Could you at least look a little dazed when we go back out? I don't want my customers to think we went back here and didn't do anything but talk."

Stanley promised that he'd try. He didn't think it would be difficult.

⌒ 39 ⌒

No Harm, No Foul

After leaving Bushwhackers, Stanley started toward Burl Cabot's auto parts store. But he stopped before he'd walked half a block. He didn't think it would be wise to go there alone, not considering the kinds of questions he was going to ask, and he wanted to make another stop first. He got into his crippled Lexus and drove to Wooded Acres.

Uncle Martin was drinking coffee and playing checkers with Goob.

"Hey, Stanley," Uncle Martin said when he saw his nephew. "You're just in time for the lizard brigade."

"The what?"

"Lizard brigade," Goob said. "You having trouble with your ears, Stanley? That's one of the first signs, they say."

"The first signs of what?"

"Old age," Goob said. "The hearing's the second thing to go."

"And you don't want us to tell you what the first thing is," Uncle Martin said. "Anyway, if it's gone, you already know."

"I can hear just fine," Stanley said. "I just didn't know what you meant by the 'lizard brigade.' "

"Wheelchair parade," Goob said. "They'll be wheeling out all the lizards in a few minutes. They're the ones that don't say much. Just sit on the porch in the sun most of the time. Somebody has to go out and move 'em every half hour or so."

"We'll be like that one of these days," Uncle Martin said cheerfully. "But not for a while yet. You get us some dates for the picture show?"

"I'm working on that."

Stanley sat down at the table and looked over the checkerboard. Two kings were sitting on the back row of Goob's side, waiting to move out and wreak havoc.

"Looks like you're winning," Stanley said to his uncle.

"Cheating's more like it," Goob said. "Asked me to get up and get some coffee for us, and then he rearranged the board."

"Did not," Uncle Martin said.

"Did so," Goob told him.

Stanley interrupted before they could get started good. Once they got worked up, they could go on for quite a while.

"Never mind. Forget the checker game for a minute. I think both of you have been guilty of something, and it doesn't have anything to do with checkers."

The two men looked at each other and then at Stanley.

"What do you mean by that?" Uncle Martin said.

"I mean I asked you to do something, and I don't think you did it."

"What might that be?" Goob said.

"You remember when I came out here the other day and talked to you about Burl Cabot, Duffy Weeks, Al Walker, and a few other people?"

Uncle Martin and Goob said that they remembered.

"And do you remember that when I left, I asked you to keep everything we'd talked about confidential?"

"Sure we remember," Uncle Martin said. "Nothing wrong with our minds, not yet. We're not lizards by a long shot."

"Well, I don't think you did."

"Did what?" Goob asked.

"Did keep everything confidential."

"We sure did," Goob said. "We didn't tell a soul."

"Are you sure?"

Uncle Martin was looking down at the checkerboard. Goob started tapping the fingers of his right hand on the tabletop.

"Let me put it this way," Stanley said. "You both like Lacy Falk. She comes out here to cut hair, and she likes to talk. Has she been out here lately?"

"Nope," Uncle Martin said. "She comes around the first of the month. That's a week or so off."

Stanley felt something inside him relax just a little. He'd been pretty sure that Lacy wasn't the person he was looking for, but he'd had to ask the question. Now he could ask an even more important one.

"What about Burl Cabot's mother?"

Goob's fingers danced a little faster. Uncle Martin looked at the TV set as if fascinated by a woman who was guessing the price of a refrigerator.

"You talked to her, didn't you?" Stanley said.

Uncle Martin turned from the TV set. "Well, hell. She's his mother. What harm would it do to say something to her about it?"

Hardly any harm at all, Stanley thought. Unless you count nearly getting me killed.

ᐵ 40 ᐸ

Live on Tape

Stanley didn't really think he'd nearly been killed, though it had seemed close enough to it at the time. He left Wooded Acres and headed for the police station. He still wanted to talk to Burl, but now he was pretty sure that he'd better talk to Marilyn first. Besides, he had another reason for stopping by the station.

Johnetta Lively was the dispatcher. Stanley asked her if he could see Marilyn.

"Chief Tunney's in her office, but she can't be disturbed." Johnetta's voice had a slight quiver that surprised Stanley. Johnetta wasn't the nervous type.

"I think I'll just walk on back and check."

"You can't do that." Stanley ignored Johnetta. After all, what could she do to him? Arrest him? She wasn't even a sworn officer.

Marilyn was in her office. She was eating a jelly-filled doughnut, and a cup of coffee sat among the papers on her desk.

Brad Bridger was there, too, with his own coffee cup and his own doughnut. It was a plain glazed.

"Stanley," Marilyn said. "What are you doing here?"

"I came to talk to you about Rance Wofford's murder," Stanley said, looking at Bridger. "But I can see that you're busy."

"That's right, Waters," Bridger said. "She's busy, and we've already caught the perp in that case. We have a confession and everything. We're the professionals here. So why don't you run along and work out a five-day forecast or something and leave the police work to us."

Stanley thought about mentioning that he, and not the professionals, was the one who'd brought Duffy in, but he didn't think it was worth it.

"Do you really believe that Duffy Weeks killed Wofford?" Stanley asked instead.

"You're damned right I do," Bridger said. "Those videotapes we have will prove it, too. They'll show he was in the right position to have fired the shot, and when the FBI lab gets those two tapes analyzed, we'll have him dead to rights even without the confession. So we don't need you to confuse the issue."

"I'm not trying to confuse the issue. I'm trying to clarify it. Marilyn, do you have copies of those tapes that we could look at right now?"

"Yes. But Brad's right, Stanley. We don't have to look at them. We know who shot Wofford."

"Could you let me see them anyway? As a personal favor?"

"No," Bridger said. "Now move it along, Waters."

Stanley stood his ground. "I wasn't aware that you'd been promoted to chief."

Bridger stood up. He set his coffee cup and half-eaten doughnut on Marilyn's desk. He smiled at Stanley. "I think I'll indulge in a little police brutality."

Stanley hoped he wasn't about to get into another fight. Considering everything that had happened lately, he wondered if maybe he should take some self-defense classes.

"That's enough, Brad," Marilyn said. "You were about to investigate the robbery at the hardware store, and you might as well get to work on it."

Bridger acted as if he couldn't believe what he was hearing. "But this guy is harassing you."

"I think I can handle it. You go do your job."

Stanley stepped aside as Bridger moved sulkily out of the room. He was sure Bridger had been about to bump him, and he didn't want a confrontation in front of Marilyn. Maybe that would come later, though it wasn't anything that Stanley looked forward to.

"Do you really want to see those tapes?" Marilyn asked.

"Yes, if you don't mind."

"Come on, then."

Marilyn took him to a room with no windows. It had seven folding chairs, along with a monitor and a VCR on a stand. Several tapes were stacked on top of a cabinet, and Marilyn looked through them before selecting two and holding them up.

"Here they are. Which one do you want to see?"

"Both of them. From the beginning."

Marilyn turned off the overhead lights, leaving on a small lamp at the back of the room, and started the first tape.

The tapes had been made by two separate cameramen, one of whom had been concentrating almost exclusively on Stanley and the men near him. Stanley had already seen part of that tape. The other tape had been taken of the Union soldiers and the men who had gotten behind them.

What Stanley had missed on his first viewing was the men who were loading their guns and firing all around him before charging out of the trees. That was on the first tape, and it was eerie to see it all again, especially when they got to the part where Rance Wofford gave his rebel yell.

"That's far enough." Stanley didn't feel any special need to see himself getting shot again. In fact, he really didn't think he wanted to see that at all.

"Did you see something I missed? I hope not because I've watched it at least ten times, looking for some kind of clue."

"There aren't any clues. I was just hoping to see Duffy loading his gun."

"It's not on there."

"I know. But you did notice him slipping off to get behind the Union troops, didn't you?"

"Yes," Marilyn said. "So?"

"He didn't fire his rifle at all. He just left."

"That's right. He didn't fire until later. We have that on the other tape."

"Good. Let's watch that one."

Marilyn put the second tape in the VCR and started it. Stanley watched the whole thing, which didn't take long. Then he asked Marilyn to run it again.

"You saw something, didn't you," she said. "If there's something there, why didn't I see it?"

"You didn't know what to look for."

"But you'll tell me, won't you?"

"Sure. Run the tape one more time."

Marilyn rewound the tape and pressed PLAY. The scene started again.

"See?" Stanley said. "There come the rebs out of the trees behind the Union boys. Duffy and Burl and Al. Neddy's a little bit behind them."

"I can see that. Nothing unusual so far."

"Except for Duffy. You can tell he's a little unsteady on his feet."

"He'd been drinking. Early in the morning, and he'd already had a few."

"He'd had a few the night before, too," Stanley said. "He's been drinking a lot. Everybody's talked about it."

Marilyn nodded. "But what does that have to do with anything?"

"It's probably the reason he falls down. Right about . . . now."

On the screen, Duffy, Burl, and Al were running practically shoulder to shoulder. Duffy plunged forward and fell to his knees in the grass. Al went on by, but Burl bent down to help Duffy.

Burl put his rifle down and pulled Duffy to his feet. They picked up their rifles, and Burl said something to Duffy. Then Burl ran on, but Duffy dropped back down into firing position and shot his rifle.

"That's just about when Rance Wofford was hit," Marilyn said. "The FBI will confirm it for us. We can place both Duffy and Wofford precisely, and that way we can determine if the bullet was fired from Duffy's gun. With the confession, we'll have all we need to convict Duffy of the murder. Is that what you wanted to see?"

"That's what I wanted to see. You can turn off the VCR now. And then I have one more favor to ask."

"What's that?"

"I want you to go shopping for a radiator with me."

"A radiator? What kind? To heat a room at the inn or to put on a car?"

"To put on a car. I had a little accident."

"I don't remember seeing a report on it."

"There was no report. But it happened all the same. Wait till you see my car."

"And you want me to help you find a replacement radiator? Why?"

"For one thing, I have a few more things to tell you on the way over to the auto parts store. And for another, you're the one with the gun."

⌒ 41 ⌒

Radiating Accusations

Betty Cabot was working the cash register at Cabot's Auto Parts. She was short, with blue eyes and dark brown hair, a combination that Stanley had always liked. She had a sweet smile, and Stanley was glad to see no sign of any bruises on her face.

"Hi, Betty," he said. "Where's Burl?"

"Hi, Stanley. Hi, Chief Tunney. Burl's in back. He's putting some mufflers in stock. Can I help you?"

"I wanted to talk to him about a radiator. Can I just go on back and talk to him?"

"Sure. He'll be glad to get you a radiator if you need one. We don't stock them, though. He'll have to order it from Alexandria."

"That's all right. I think mine will get me through the day. How do we get to the back?"

Betty came out from behind the counter and showed them the door that led to the storage area. Stanley and Marilyn went through and saw Burl Cabot standing beside a stack of mufflers while he checked off numbers on an invoice attached to a brown clipboard. The wide delivery door was open, and Stanley could see across the parking lot to the dress shop on the other side of the street.

"Hey, Burl," Stanley said. "Got a new shipment?"

Burl Cabot looked around. When he saw Stanley and Marilyn, he put the clipboard down on the stack of mufflers and smiled.

"Good morning, Stanley. Chief Tunney. Come to buy some auto parts today?"

Stanley told him that he needed a radiator for the Lexus.

"That's a special order item," Burl said. "But I can get it for you. You going to install it yourself?"

"I think I'll get someone to do that for me. And I'll need some bodywork, too."

"Ed Clark's a good body man. He'll treat you right, too."

"I'll give him a call," Stanley said. "By the way, did you ever find out who took a shot at you the other day?"

Burl looked at Marilyn. "I haven't been looking. That's the police's job."

"Stanley tells me we aren't going to find anyone," Marilyn said.

"Why not?" Burl asked.

"Because there wasn't anyone," Stanley said.

Burl picked up the clipboard. "I don't know what you're trying to pull, Stanley, but I don't have time for it. I have work to do."

"I think this might be more important than your work," Marilyn said. "Stanley has a theory that I'd like you to hear."

Burl put down the clipboard. "I'll listen. But make it quick."

"It won't take long," Stanley said. "The other day when you supposedly got shot, you said that someone came by in a black car. A shot was fired, and you hit the floor. Is that about right?"

"I guess so. I don't really remember."

"I do," Marilyn told him. "That's what you said."

Burl shrugged. "Okay, so I said it. So what?"

Stanley looked down at the floor. Oil and grease stained it, and it obviously hadn't been swept in days. Weeks maybe.

"When I saw you right after the shooting," Stanley said, "your jeans were just as neat as they are now. Not a spot on them. You didn't hit the floor. And I don't think anyone shot at you, either. If they did, no one heard the shot. I talked to Jane Gray. She heard the siren and the police cars, but she didn't hear any shot."

"You're forgetting one thing," Burl said. "There was a bullet in a muffler right over there."

"I know," Stanley said. "That bothered me for a while, but I decided that you fired the bullet into the muffler yourself, probably not here but out in the country somewhere. Then you brought the muffler back here, still in the box."

"That's ridiculous. Why would I do something like that?"

"Because you wanted to divert suspicion from yourself," Stanley said. "I'd been attacked, and you didn't want anyone to think you'd done it. So you made up that story about being shot at, hoping the police would think I wasn't the only one being attacked."

"That's a bunch of bull."

"No, it's not. You're the one who came out to the inn and chased me around in a black car, and you're the one who took a few shots at me and Marilyn, not to mention your own muffler. If anyone had been trying to eliminate all the people connected with Wofford's shooting, there would have been attempts on Al Walker or Neddy Drake. But there haven't been. Just on you and me."

Burl shook his head sadly. "Stanley, I don't know what you've been smoking, but I'd have to guess that it's not a legal substance. I didn't do those things."

"Sure you did. You visited your mother in Wooded Acres, and she told you that I'd been asking questions. I hate to seem immodest, but you'd heard people talking about me and my, ah, investigative abilities, and you wanted to scare me. So you gave it a try. It didn't work the first time, so you tried again, after another visit to your mother. Both those attacks happened after I'd been to Wooded Acres and talked things over with my uncle Martin, who told your mother about my visits. And she told you."

Burl was looking puzzled, or trying to. "Why would I attack you, Stanley? I didn't have any reason to worry about your investigation; I didn't do anything."

"Yes, you did. You killed Rance Wofford."

Burl laughed. "Now I know you've been smoking those funny cigarettes. Either that, or you've been drinking. Half the town knows by now that Duffy Weeks killed Rance. He's even admitted it. Isn't that right, Chief Tunney?"

"That's right. Or it's right that Duffy's confessed. But Stanley says Duffy didn't kill anyone."

"That's right," Stanley said. "Duffy had a motive, all right, but so did you. So did a lot of people. But you're the only one who's been trying to scare me."

Burl picked up his clipboard and looked down at the invoice. Then he looked at Stanley. "I think you're nuts. I guess it was interesting to hear what you had to say, but I have a store to run here. If Duffy says he killed Wofford, that's good enough for me, and it'll be good enough for a jury, too."

"Maybe not," Stanley said. "Not after they see the videotapes."

Burl put his clipboard down again. "What videotapes?"

"The ones the *Hello, World!* crew was making," Marilyn said. "I have copies of them at the station."

"Those were on TV. They didn't show anything."

"They do, though," Stanley said. "They show you bumping into Duffy and knocking him off-balance."

"Duffy had been drinking. That's why he fell down."

"He'd been drinking, all right," Stanley said. "And you did a good job of making it look as if he fell. But he didn't. You bumped him. His drinking made it easier for you, I'm sure. It made it easier for you to do something else, too."

"And I'm sure you'll tell me what that was."

"Yes, I will. You switched rifles with him."

It is the mountaintop
that the lightning strikes.

—Horace, *Odes*, 1.10

My heart leaps up when I behold
A rainbow in the sky.

—Wordsworth, "My Heart Leaps Up"

⤜ 42 ⤛

The Chased and the Unchased

"You can't see that on any tape," Burl said.

"Not very easily," Stanley admitted. "You put down the rifle you were carrying, and it's concealed by the grass."

"Even if the switch were true, you couldn't prove it."

"That's where you're wrong," Stanley said. "If it's true, the FBI computer enhancement of the tape should show that you picked up Duffy's rifle. Or, that is, you picked up your own. The other rifle, which you had loaded with a minié ball, was Duffy's, which you had switched for yours earlier that morning. He'd had too much to drink to notice the switch. And I think the enhancement will show even more. The FBI has experienced lip-readers. They'll be able to tell what you said to Duffy when you helped him up. I imagine it was something like, 'Let's shoot Wofford, Duffy, just the way we talked about.' "

"None of that happened. Even if it did, Duffy still pulled the trigger."

"I know," Stanley said. "It's going to make for an interesting trial."

Just then the door opened behind Stanley and Marilyn. Stanley looked around. Betty Cabot was standing there.

"It's sure taking you a long time to find out about that radiator," Betty said.

"They don't want any radiator," Burl said. "They're going to arrest me for killing Wofford."

"No, they're not," Betty said.

She pulled a box of spark plugs off the shelf and threw it at Marilyn's head. Marilyn dodged, and the box glanced off her shoulder.

Stanley wasn't so lucky. The muffler box that Burl threw hit him right in the face. Stanley staggered backward, his head ringing. He bumped into Marilyn, who fell right into Betty's arms.

Betty hugged Marilyn to her and yelled, "I've got her, Burl! Run!"

Burl ran out of the building toward the parking lot. Stanley had recovered enough to try to help Marilyn, but Marilyn didn't want any help.

"You go after Burl," she said. "I'll handle this."

Stanley wasn't so sure. Betty had dragged Marilyn to the floor and was hanging on to her as Marilyn squirmed to get free. But if he hesitated any longer, Burl was going to be long gone. So Stanley took off after him.

After about the first five yards, Stanley was convinced of one thing: he didn't like chasing any more than he liked being chased. He was already wheezing like a leaky accordion.

Across the street, Jane Gray was standing outside her dress shop, looking in Stanley's direction. He wanted to yell to her and tell her to stop Burl, but he was afraid that if he yelled, he'd have to stop running and catch his breath, so he didn't yell. He just kept running.

By the time Stanley got into the middle of the parking lot, Burl was already at the street. Jane Gray walked over as if to ask him what was going on, but she didn't get a chance. Burl stiff-armed her, and she sat down hard on the sidewalk, a look of surprise and pain on her face.

Stanley didn't stop to help her up, and he didn't slow down to say that he was sorry. Burl had turned the corner at Bush-whackers, and Stanley was more worried about losing his quarry than he was about Jane's tailbone.

There was a loud yell from around the corner, and Stanley sped up. He wouldn't have thought he was capable of additional speed, but the yell brought a little burst of adrenaline from somewhere that had never been called on before.

When Stanley turned the corner, he saw Burl doing a sort of do-si-do with Pearl Williams, who had no doubt done the yelling and whose husband owned a jewelry store just down the street. Every time that Pearl moved left, Burl moved right. If Pearl moved right, Burl moved left. He couldn't get around her, and Stanley would have laughed if he'd only had the breath to do it with.

Burl looked over his shoulder and saw Stanley barreling toward him. He didn't try to dodge Pearl again. He reached out one of his immense hands and shoved her backward as hard as he could.

Pearl's mouth opened in amazement, and one of her heels caught on a rough patch of sidewalk. She threw up her arms and barely had time to yell again before her broad back struck the glass window that fronted Bushwhackers.

Stanley could see the astonished faces of Lacy's customers just before they scattered.

The glass cracked with a sound like a rifle shot and cracks spiderwebbed it. Stanley jumped forward with more alacrity than he would have thought he had in him and grabbed Pearl's hand, jerking her toward him. As he yanked, the glass fragmented and showered into the shop and onto the sidewalk.

Everyone in the shop was screaming, but Burl Cabot didn't stick around to see if anyone was hurt. He was already half a block away.

Stanley let go of Pearl's hand and started off after Burl. The brief breather hadn't done much to restore his lung power, but as he passed Grove's Drug and the Super Food Store, he thought he might be gaining a little. Burl was even bigger than Stanley, and, Stanley told himself, he certainly wasn't in better shape.

Still, Stanley might never have caught him if it hadn't been for Tommy Bright, who was out riding the Columbia bicycle that Stanley coveted.

To be on the safe side, Tommy was keeping out of the traffic by riding the bike on the sidewalk, which was against a Higgins city ordinance that was widely ignored by everyone in Higgins under the age of twelve. Tommy hadn't seen the age of twelve in forty years, but that didn't seem to be bothering him as he cruised dreamily along.

Stanley saw Tommy almost as soon as Burl did and decided to take a chance on yelling at him.

"Tommy! Don't let Burl get away!"

Tommy looked up, seeing Burl and Stanley for the first time. Instead of trying to stop Burl, he tried to swerve out of the way.

He didn't make it.

It was the do-si-do all over again, but this time both Burl and Tommy were moving too fast for any "after you, Alphonse" routine.

Burl collided with the bicycle, which came to a sudden and immediate stop, with Tommy flying over the handlebars and slamming headfirst into Burl.

When Stanley arrived at the scene, Burl, Tommy, and the bicycle were all three lying in a tangled heap on the sidewalk. The bicycle's front wheel had sustained heavy damage. Most of the spokes were bent because, unfortunately, Burl Cabot had stuck his foot through the wheel, and the wheel was twisted at an odd angle. The tank was scraped, and the headlight was broken.

Stanley sighed. He'd really liked that bicycle.

⌐ 43 ⌐

Busted

Stanley was helping Tommy to his feet when Brad Bridger drove up in an unmarked car that squealed to a stop beside the curb.

Bridger jumped out of the car as if he were performing for the cameras of *N.Y.P.D. Blue*. He drew his pistol, gripped it with both hands, and pointed it at Burl Cabot's head.

Stanley was sure that Burl didn't care. Tommy had been wearing a bike rider's safety helmet. Burl hadn't, of course, and he'd been rendered instantly unconscious when the helmet struck him in the head. He lay on the sidewalk like a crash-test dummy.

"You're busted, dirtbag," Bridger said. "Don't move."

There didn't appear to be much danger of that. Stanley doubted that Burl could even hear what Bridger was saying.

"For God's sake, don't shoot him," Tommy said. "Reckless running isn't a capital crime, is it? And I want him alive to pay for that bicycle. I was testing it for a customer, and this is going to cost me a sale."

"Burl's wanted for more than ruining your bike," Stanley said. "He's got something a lot worse on his conscience, and I think Brad wants credit for the arrest. He's already taken credit for Duffy, but he had the wrong man."

"Can it," Bridger said. "You two citizens can clear out. The professionals have things well in hand here."

"Well, of course you do," Tommy said, nudging Burl with the toe of one Dexter walking shoe. "Anyone can see that Burl's not putting up any resistance."

"Where's Marilyn?" Stanley asked Bridger.

Bridger didn't take his eyes off Burl. It was as if Brad was afraid Burl would suddenly leap up and disarm him if he relaxed his vigilance. To Stanley, Burl didn't appear capable of disarming Little Bo-peep.

"You deserted Marilyn, Waters," Bridger said. "I'll discuss that with you later."

"I didn't desert anyone. I was chasing a criminal. The one you're holding a gun on."

"That's your story."

"You might as well give it up," Tommy told Stanley. "He's not in a reasonable state of mind. Do you think he'll kill Burl?"

"He'd better not," Stanley said. "Where's Marilyn, Brad?"

"Taking her prisoner to jail. Now go away."

Stanley looked at Tommy, who shrugged. "Let's go. I can get the bike later. Though I shudder to think what the repair bill will be. And I've lost the sale, of course."

Quite a little crowd had gathered, and Stanley and Tommy were asked all kinds of questions as they made their way through it. One of them was "Who shot out the window in Bushwhackers?"

Stanley didn't answer any of the questions, but he did walk back by Bushwhackers to check on Lacy, who was fine. So were all her customers, though the same couldn't be said for her front window.

"It's a wonder someone wasn't killed," Lacy said. "It's thanks to you that Pearl Williams got away without getting cut to pieces. You've got fast hands, Stanley."

Nearly everything that Lacy said seemed to Stanley to have two or three meanings, none of which he had any desire to analyze too thoroughly.

"What was that all about, anyway?" Lacy asked. "Half my

customers are down the street right now, trying to see what's going on."

"There was a bicycle accident," Stanley said.

Stanley walked to the police station. Johnetta greeted him and said that he could go on back to Chief Tunney's office.

Marilyn was sitting at her desk. Grease from Cabot's floor was on her blouse and several scratches were on her face.

"I take it that you didn't have too much trouble with Betty," Stanley said.

"More than I wanted. But she gave in pretty easily after Burl took off."

Stanley sat down and stretched his legs out in front of him. His calf muscles were getting a little tight.

"I didn't expect her to come back there while we were talking," he said.

"Well, there's more to the story than you know. For one thing, the shooting was her idea."

Stanley didn't jump out of his chair, but his mouth did drop open.

"You seem surprised. I thought you had things all figured out."

Stanley had thought so, too. And Betty didn't figure into anything he'd come up with.

"I must have missed something," he said. "Did she tell you that she suggested the shooting?"

"Yes. How else would I know? Anyway, it was mostly her idea."

"I don't get it. You're going to have to explain it to me."

Marilyn smiled. "Well, well. The internationally famed investigator admits that he has some limitations."

Stanley knew he shouldn't have said anything about Burl being afraid of Stanley's investigative abilities, not in front of Marilyn at any rate.

"I have plenty of limitations," he said. "I'll admit that I thought I had it all figured out, but apparently I was overconfident."

"Don't feel too bad about it. You were close. But you did

draw one wrong conclusion. Remember those bruises that Lacy told you about?"

Stanley said that he remembered.

"Well, Burl didn't put them there."

Stanley started to say that Lacy had told him differently, but when he thought it over, he remembered that actually she hadn't. Both she and Stanley had assumed that Burl had made the bruises, but Betty had never said so.

"Okay," Stanley said. "If Burl didn't hit her, I can guess who did. Wofford."

Marilyn straightened some of the papers on her desk, tapped them into line, then looked at Stanley.

"Now you're on the right track. Wofford came to town and sort of swept her off her feet. She married Burl right out of high school, never had any big romance other than that, and she's been right here in Higgins for her entire life. Along comes a rich man from the big city and puts the moves on her, tells her what she's been missing, and promises to deliver it all. Naturally she responded."

Stanley listened not only to Marilyn's words but her tone, mainly because there was at least a slight parallel between Betty's story and what had happened between Marilyn and Stanley. But the parallel was only slight. Very slight. That made a difference. Or Stanley hoped it did.

"Wofford showed her a great time, at first," Marilyn continued, as if unaware of any underlying implications in what she was saying. "And then he became more and more insistent about Burl selling out to him. It finally dawned on Betty that Wofford was hoping to use her to get what he wanted from her husband."

Stanley wasn't surprised. Wofford had resorted to a detective to find a way to put the squeeze on Duffy. He wouldn't be above handing out plenty of malarkey to a woman to put the squeeze on her husband. But it hadn't worked.

"And Betty eventually told Wofford what she thought of him," Stanley said.

"That's right. Colorfully and at length, I believe. Wofford's response was a bit more violent than she had any reason to expect."

"He was a vicious guy," Stanley said, thinking again of Wofford's approach to Duffy. "In more ways than one."

"You could say that. But he made an error in judgment. He didn't think Betty would have the nerve to tell Burl what had happened."

"Obviously she did."

"She did. Burl was going to beat Wofford to a pulp, but Betty came up with a better idea."

Stanley still found it hard to believe and said so. He had another idea. "Maybe she's just trying to cover for Burl because she feels guilty for her involvement with Wofford."

"I don't think so. Burl would have handled things a little differently, but his solution wouldn't have been nearly as permanent. And Betty wanted something permanent. She says that she's the one who thought of using the reenactment as a cover, and when she remembered Duffy's drinking, she came up with the idea of switching the rifles. If it hadn't worked, well, there was always brute force, which Burl was certainly willing to apply."

"It worked, though, didn't it," Stanley said, running his hand gently over his stitches.

Marilyn stood up, walked around the desk, and laid her hand on Stanley's face.

"It almost worked too well," she said.

☞ 44 ☜

Triple Date

Uncle Martin was riding shotgun in Stanley's rented Ford Taurus. His overalls were clean, and his white shirt had been freshly starched and ironed.

"I never could understand a man like that Rance Wofford," Uncle Martin said. "He's successful where he is, but he doesn't stay there. He comes to a nice little town like Higgins instead, and then he screws everything up."

"Some guys get tired of being the little bitty frog in the great big pond," Goob said from the backseat. He was so small that his head wasn't visible above the package rack to drivers behind him. "Guys like him, they want to be the stud bullfrog."

"It didn't work out for Rance," Stanley said. "He tried to blend into the community, be a part of it, but he went about everything else the wrong way."

"Shouldn't ever have joined that reenactment group," Uncle Martin said. "Too dangerous."

"For some people," Goob said. "The thing is, you have to be a part of history to really understand it. People like Wofford don't get that. You do, though, don't you, Stanley?"

Stanley said that he hoped so. But that didn't mean he was going to join a reenactment group.

"You don't have to do that to be a part of history around here," Uncle Martin told him. "You were born around here. You're descended from men who were at the Battle of Higgins. The real one. And you even know that John Tyler was born in Charles City County. You're all right, Stanley."

Stanley was glad to hear it. But he had a question. "What if I hadn't been born here?"

"What difference would that make?"

"For one thing, I wouldn't be descended from someone who was at the real Battle of Higgins."

"It's not like you're FFV, Stanley," Goob said. "Don't let your ancestry go to your head."

"I wasn't. I was just asking a question."

"Well," Uncle Martin said, "the answer is that you don't have to be from here to fit in. After all, Burl and Betty are from around here, and they didn't come out of this much better than Wofford did. Being a part of something's good. Having traditions is good. But you still have to treat other people right."

"Speaking of that," Goob said, "what about these two women you lined up for us, Stanley?"

Stanley didn't want to take responsibility for the dates that had been arranged. He wasn't sure how Uncle Martin and Goob would react.

"Marilyn lined them up. They're from Higgins, so you probably know them. They're sisters, both widowed. Their maiden name was Berry, and they live together now."

"Oh, Lord," Goob said. "Franny and Belle. You remember them, Mart?"

"I sure do. They're just youngsters. They were five or six grades behind me in school, too young for me to pay any attention to, but I heard they were pretty wild back then."

Goob said that he hoped they still were. "And what's the name of this movie we're going to see?"

"*Bride of Frankenstein*," Stanley said.

"I remember that one," Goob said. "Scared me half to death first time I saw it. I'll bet that Franny Berry is sitting in my lap before it's half over."

"Hold on a minute," Uncle Martin said. "What makes you think you'll be with Franny?"

"She's the older one, and I'm older than you. I get to do the picking."

"Maybe the women have some ideas of their own," Stanley said before the argument could gain any momentum. "We'll find out when we get to the theater. Marilyn's bringing them to meet us there."

"What about her and that Brad Bridger?" Uncle Martin asked. "Has she figured out what a phony he is yet?"

"I think maybe she has," Stanley said. "I didn't know it myself until I had a few dealings with him, but he's just Officer Kunkel with better hair."

"What about you and Lacy Falk, Stanley?" Uncle Martin asked. "I heard today that you'd been sparking her."

"I wouldn't say that. We get along all right, though."

"What does Chief Tunney think about that?"

Stanley didn't know, and he wasn't going to ask. He liked Lacy, but his feelings for Marilyn went a bit deeper than liking. If she hadn't caught on to Bridger yet, she soon would. He didn't mind waiting.

"And you've solved another murder for her," Goob said. "Of course you had our help, and that made a big difference. Anyhow, I guess that means you'll be doing some more detective work."

Stanley grinned. He didn't know whether Marilyn would ask him to help out again or not, and he might not find out for a while. He hoped that sooner or later she'd see that he made a pretty good unofficial assistant and that even when he was personally involved in a case, he could see it through without getting hurt. Well, not hurt too badly.

But he didn't want to go into all that with Uncle Martin and Goob.

"We'll see what happens," was all he said.

Afterword

The weather, be it fair or foul, has always been a fascinating topic of discourse, and writers throughout the centuries have referred to it in their work. They have used it to comment on character, to establish the tone of a story or a poem, or to reinforce a theme. Some of their words have become common parlance, while others are less well known. We hope that you've enjoyed seeing some of them reprinted in this book.